TAMPICO TRAUMA

A JAKE SULLIVAN NOVEL

THE JAKE SULLIVAN SERIES

Come Monday

Trying to Reason with Hurricane Season

Havana Daydreamin'

A Pirate Looks at Forty

One Particular Harbour

Son of a Son of a Sailor

Jamaica Mistaica

Changes in Latitudes, Changes in Attitudes

He Went to Paris

Tampico Trauma

ALSO AVAILABLE:

Trilogy

COMING FALL 2017:

Fins

TAMPICO TRAUMA

A JAKE SULLIVAN NOVEL

CHIP BELL

WORD ASSOCIATION PUBLISHERS
www.wordassociation.com
1.800.827.7903

Printed in the United States of America.

ISBN: 978-1-63385-168-9

Library of Congress Control Number: 2017905942

Designed and published by

Word Association Publishers
205 Fifth Avenue
Tarentum, Pennsylvania 15084

www.wordassociation.com
1.800.827.7903

"I must look like a mess I must admit
But I have been traveling quite a bit
South of the border where the law and order
Is kept by Federales who just grin."

- "Tampico Trauma"
by Jimmy Buffett

DEDICATION

To all the wonderful people I have met since I started on this journey.

ACKNOWLEDGEMENT

To Eve, always, for all her hard work, and to April and Jason at Word Association, who are always there when I need them.

PROLOGUE

SAN CARLOS DE BARILOCHE ARGENTINA

1954

CHAPTER 1

Even though it was just past noon and the sun reflected brilliantly off the shores of Lake Nahuel Huapi, all was dark in the offices of Gunselman Art Dealers International, advertised by the bronze plaque near its front door as "Buyers and Sellers of Art and Artifacts".

Two men, one angry and the other trying to placate that anger, both with gray hair and imposing demeanors, were seated at opposite sides of a huge Victorian desk in a well-appointed office. Behind that desk sat Stephan Gunselman, and across from him a man dressed in a tweed suit, with wire-rimmed glasses.

"You have no choice here, Gunselman. I've verified things with our people in Israel. The Mossad is here, in Bariloche. They've picked up the scent."

The man behind the desk slammed his fist down and spoke through a rage.

"You were supposed to prevent this from happening. Are you telling me that all of the safeguards we created were not enough?! You know very well what will happen if the Jews take me! I will tell them everything . . . and you know that I know everything!"

"I suggest you calm down. You're in no position to make threats, my friend. We gave you a new life and saved you from a horrible death. You have been able to spend your later years involved in your true passion."

In response, Herr Gunselman leaned across the desk.

"And what have I given? And was it not I who created the international network we use for the shipment and transfer of weapons and other goods? Is it not Die Spinne, led by Skorzeny, that has become your team of assassins? And isn't it ODESSA and its escape routes and organization that we have used to amplify our international contacts? You have all this because of me! They all report to me! They exist because of me! And their loyalty is to me!"

The gentleman across the desk remained calm and leaned back, tenting his fingers in front of him.

"There is no question that you have provided a valuable service and that the organizations of which you speak have been crucial to our undertakings," and then he leaned forward, "but that is why you must be calm and listen. I am here to help you . . . for the very reasons you have just stated. We have made arrangements through Perón and his relationship with Cortines . . . and we will relocate you. The trail will end here, in Bariloche. We erect another wall for the Mossad to run into . . . just as we have in the past. You will be set up exactly as you are here, except with a new name."

Just then, there was a knock at the door, and a young man, age fourteen or fifteen, stuck his head through the opening.

"Excuse me, father."

"Come in, Alios . . . come in. Say hello to Mr. Trent. You have not seen him for some time."

"Hello, Alios. How are you?"

"Fine, Mr. Trent. I am sorry to disturb your meeting."

"That's fine, Alios. What is it?"

"Do you want all the new crates opened . . . or only the ones from the Balkans?"

"The Balkan crates only, Alios. They must be made ready for shipment to Lebanon immediately."

"I'll see to it, father."

"Thank you, my son."

"Nice seeing you, Mr. Trent."

"You, also, Alios."

The man called Trent looked across the desk and smiled.

"I see you now have a family business."

"He is a good boy. Things have been difficult for him since the death of his mother," said the man behind the desk as he rose and stood before the window, looking out over the square and the lake. He had calmed down. His anger was spent. And without turning, he asked, "Where?"

"On the coast, along the Gulf . . . Tampico. A beautiful villa and an office near the port. I have never been there, but I have heard it is a beautiful city that resembles New Orleans."

The man at the window held up his hand.

"Enough!" And said, almost to himself, "And now I am to become a Mexican."

LOS PINOS
MEXICO CITY

1954

CHAPTER 2

The man standing in the office of the President of Mexico was holding a hat in his hands, wearing a white, three-piece linen suit, his bodyguards standing by the doorway. The President of Mexico, Adolfo Ruiz Cortines, was seated at his desk, shaking his head.

"You come to me asking for favors," said the President, "even though you have opposed me in the matter of the OAS. You want me to take in this person whom you call a 'refugee' but won't give me a true identity. Tell me, why should I do this?"

Juan Perón shifted the hat in his hand and looked sternly across the desk. "Have I not humbled myself? Have I not come here to you? Have I not told you that I represent a far greater entity than our governments and what that entity can do for Mexico, as it has done for Argentina?"

"Ah, yes," said the President, rising from his seat behind the desk, "the secret Group 45. Why should I believe that it even exists?"

Perón turned to one of his men and said, "Tell them to make the call," and the man withdrew from the room.

"What are we to have now," said Cortines, "a magic show?"

"Not magic, my friend. Just wait," said Perón.

Suddenly the phone rang and Perón took the receiver out of the cradle and handed it to Cortines.

21

"Who is this . . . and why should I believe you?"

Realization started to play upon his face as he sat and listened, staring at Perón the whole time, until, finally, he slowly and gently placed the receiver back in its cradle.

"Did you enjoy your conversation with Mr. Trent?"

Cortines looked up.

"You are going to get your subsidy from the Americans for the dam project, aren't you?"

Cortines just nodded.

"I assume I can expect no problems in the transfer of the package to Tampico?"

Cortines was still staring into space.

"Mr. President!" snapped Perón.

"Yes, yes . . . whatever you need. Obviously, your friend Trent has my private number. Call me if there are any difficulties."

"Thank you, Mr. President, but I assure you . . . there will be no difficulties."

And with that, Perón turned on his heel and exited. Once in the hallway, he spoke to his bodyguards.

"What a weak, little man," he said. "If I acted like that, my Presidency wouldn't have lasted a day. Come, let's get out of this horrible city and back to the beauties of Argentina."

TAMPICO, MEXICO

1976

CHAPTER 3

The room was dim, except for a small light that sat on the floor illuminating the painting on the wall. The old man, now in his 87th year, sat alone, staring at the painting of a country estate sitting in a wooded area. He's eyes, somewhat softened with age, still had a mysterious intensity to them, and he seemed to be in some sort of reverie, which was only broken when a younger person came in, pushing a wheelchair, and spoke.

"That's enough for now, father."

"Alios, this will be my last time viewing my favorite work."

"Nonsense, you have a lot of time left. Mr. Trent has promised you your own viewing space whenever the Cultural Center is built."

"Alios, they are Mexicans . . . it will be decades . . . if ever. I appreciate your kindness, son, but I've spoken with the doctor. I made them tell me. I know it's only a matter of time. I have lived 87 years and have done things that no one imagined, and had it not been for those who betrayed me, I would have conquered the world. How many men can say that? How many men get to sit alone and think while looking at their creation . . . the true love of their life, other than, of course, my son, you and your mother."

Turning in the wheelchair and taking one last look at the painting, the old man shook his head.

"No, this will be my last visit."

When they were outside the door, the young man turned and locked it and began to push the wheelchair through the large warehouse.

"Come, father," he said, returning to the wheelchair. "We'll go outside and sit in the sun. It's a beautiful day. Tomorrow, I will bring you back again."

"As you wish, Alios . . . as you wish."

WASHINGTON, D.C.

PRESENT DAY

CHAPTER 4

Jason Bates, the President's Chief of Staff, hurried from the West Wing into the conference room. He was a man of great impatience and constantly in motion, but this was the final briefing before Jake Sullivan and Mike Lang left on their quest to find Simon Branson's key, and, hopefully, the means to bring down Group 45. There were several tech assistants from White House communications, Sam Walsh, a data collector from the FBI, and an intern Bates barely recognized from the White House Travel Office.

Jake was in the middle of a conversation with Walsh and, as usual, Bates interrupted.

"So, are you guys ready? Everything in place? You think you can pull this off?"

Mike Lang, who always liked to tweak Bates when he could, spoke up.

"Sure, Jason, with all the facts at our disposal, we've come up with one hell of a plan. We're chasing a guy who is either dead or 120 years old . . . who maybe didn't die in Germany at the end of World War II . . . and maybe went to Argentina in a submarine . . . and maybe lived there until he died . . . and all that, somehow, is supposed to lead us to a computer system somewhere that holds all the information we need to bring down the evil empire. I'd say we're ready . . . wouldn't you?"

Bates just glared, and without saying a word, looked at Jake Sullivan, who was leaning on a desk with a broad grin on his face.

"Jake, can you help me out here?"

"Sam here can probably give you the details better than I can, Jason."

"Go ahead, Sam."

"Here's what we know. At the end of World War II, SMERSH, the Red Army Intelligence Agency that arrived in Berlin, allegedly found the remains of Hitler, Eva Braun, and some other Nazi higher-ups.

There have been conflicting reports since that time regarding those remains. It is on the record that the Chief of the United States Trial Council at Nuremberg, for whom, I remind you, Judge Branson worked at the time, stated that, 'No one can say that he is dead.' We know that President Truman asked Stalin point blank at the Potsdam Conference whether or not Hitler was dead, and Stalin bluntly replied, 'No.' The skull fragments that the Soviets always held out as being Hitler's were tested for DNA, but it turns out the skull plates came from a woman less than forty years of age.

The strange trip and condition of German U-Boat U-530 has been documented and could have been the vehicle that transported Hitler to Argentina. There is no question that there was a large pro-Nazi contingent living in Argentina still active at the end of the war, particularly in the Patagonian region at the foothills of the Andes.

As you all know, there have been sightings and rumors, documentaries produced, and books written, placing Hitler at various places and having various identities. But, if, in fact, he did escape and did make it to Argentina, having sifted through all of the information, the best place to begin the search would be in Bariloche, and specifically, the Villa La Angostura on the shores of Lake Nahuel Huapi, approximately eighty miles north.

As you can see on this map," Walsh pointed to as he rose from his seat and moved to a white board hung on the wall, "aerial photographs show a residence, set amid a pine forest, and it appears that it can only be reached by boat or hydroplane. We know it belonged at the time to an Argentine businessman named Antonio, one of Perón's most trusted henchmen."

"Okay," said Bates, "I get it. So that maybe is the house where Hitler lived. But, as Mr. Lang so sarcastically informed us, the guy's been dead for years."

"You're right, Jason," said Jake, "but it's a starting point. Hopefully, we'll find people who can give us some information. If I'm right, and if Hitler was recruited to work for Group 45, Simon Branson came to know about it. And the strange references he made . . . about Hitler's paintings and other things . . . what can I tell you, Jason, it's just my gut."

"That sounds familiar. It's a place to start. I'm sure the President will be happy to hear that we're working on your gut instinct again."

"The results haven't been too bad so far," said Mike.

"I know, I know," said Bates, holding up his hand. "I understand. All right, it's a go. Coordinate everything you need to coordinate. And please . . . keep me posted."

Bates was up and gone as his sentence trailed off behind him, heading for the Oval Office to brief the President.

CHAPTER 5

President Jordan Fletcher was still sitting behind the Resolute Desk, deep in thought, with Jason Bates standing before him.

"I just don't know, Jason. Maybe it's all a fantasy . . . one of those crazy hoaxes that evolved over time . . . and everyone now thinks it's truth, but it really isn't."

"I understand your concern, sir, but as Lang reminded me, these guys have been awful good about following their gut instincts."

"I know," said the President, "they've had great success, but it's a matter of time, Jason. Group 45 isn't going to stop. You're sure there is nowhere else we could concentrate our resources more valuably than this?"

"I'm afraid not, sir. We have no leads. We don't know if the recordings of Simon Branson were the rantings of a crazy and dying man, or if they had substance, but he told Jake to follow the package . . . and Jake is sure the package was Hitler."

The President rose and put his hands in his pants' pockets, as he always did when he made a decision.

"All right . . . it's a go. Hopefully, they'll be able to pull off another one."

"Yes, sir," said Bates. "And, Mr. President, the party you've been waiting for is now outside."

"Wonderful . . . send him in . . . send him in. Thank you, Jason."

Bates exited the Oval Office and turned to the man sitting in full dress Naval uniform.

"He'll see you now."

And the man entered the Oval Office, coming to a brisk salute as he stood before the President of the United States.

"Welcome, Commander. At ease . . . at ease. Sit down. There is something I need you to do for me . . . you and your team."

"Anything, sir," said Commander Brett Donahower, taking a seat and listening as the President gave him his orders.

CHAPTER 6

Back in the conference room, Jake and Mike were talking with Stanley Cashman, a technical specialist from White House Communications.

"All right, this phone works along the same lines as the British Codex. Everything is completely encrypted, all your contacts have been downloaded into the phone, it has a homing signal you can activate," he said, pushing another button, "worldwide GPS, and this red button is your direct line to Bates and the Oval Office."

"We'll try not to touch that one," said Mike, smiling at Jake.

"And this," said Cashman, "is the most important piece of equipment I have for you," he said while opening his hand and showing a flash drive. "If we're all correct, what you ultimately are going to find is a high-tech computer system storing all the data we are looking for and it will have a USB port. If we do get to that moment in time, you push the green button on your phone and you'll be instantly connected with me, and only me, 24-7, at which time I will have you insert this flash drive into the USB port and that will start a download of all data on the system. Once the download is completed, I will destroy the hard drive in such a fashion that no one will be able to reconstruct it, and it will solely be ours. So, please, don't lose this," he said, holding out his hand to Jake, who took the flash drive.

"Got it. Consider it done."

"I wish I was as optimistic as you are about all this, Mr. Sullivan."

"You've got to have faith," said Mike, slapping Cashman on the back. "Don't worry, we just make this stuff up as we go along. We'll find it."

Cashman looked at Mike, who was grinning broadly, and just shook his head, not knowing what to say.

Next up was the young intern, Samantha Brewer, from the White House Travel Office, who explained the arrangements that had been made for their trip to Argentina.

"Your flight on Azul Airlines will leave Fort Lauderdale at 8:45 P.M., tomorrow and arrive at Sao Paulo, Brazil, at 5:55 A.M., for a nine-hour first leg of your trip. Your next flight on Aerolineas Argentinas leaves at 10:30 A.M., and arrives in Buenos Aires at 1:25 P.M. There will be a car waiting to pick you up to take you to the Embassy at 1300 Columbia Avenue in Buenos Aires. Embassy personnel will take over travel arrangements from there, which I'm afraid are classified above my pay grade."

"Thank you, Samantha," said Jake. "We appreciate it."

She nodded and smiled at both of them and exited the room.

"Well," said Mike, folding his arms and leaning against the table. "I guess we're all set. Another impossible mission. You know, maybe we should start our own movie series when we're done."

"And let me guess," said Jake, heading to the door without looking back, "you want Tom Cruise to play you."

Mike followed him out.

"I think there are certain similarities."

MIAMI, FLORIDA

CHAPTER 7

Back in the office in Miami, Jake and Mike had just put the finishing touches on the memos to those who would be taking care of things while they were away. Jake had a long conversation with Eva, knowing full well that she would take care of the office better than he could. As usual, she said goodbye in her own way.

"You two take care of each other . . . and don't make me come down there."

After she was gone, Mike looked at Jake.

"Why do I get the feeling that she'd be better at this than we are?"

"Because she probably would," said Jake.

Finishing up, they agreed that Mike would pick Jake up at his home and head out to the airport for their flight later that evening.

"Sounds good. I'll see you in a couple of hours. I'm going home and spend some time with Linda before I have to leave again. We're going to call the girls and see if I can get in at least a little bit of family time."

"Say hello to everybody for me," said Mike.

"You got it."

Mike was heading out the door when he turned and looked at Jake.

"All the goodbyes . . . never knowing what's going to happen . . . you sometimes wonder why we keep doing this?"

Without hesitation, Jake replied, "Because it has to be done, and because we can."

Mike didn't respond. He just nodded, turned, and waved, and he was gone.

SAO PAULO, BRAZIL
AND
BUENOS AIRES,
ARGENTINA

CHAPTER 8

The flight from Lauderdale had left on time and they were making their approach to Sao Paulo, Brazil, to await the next leg of their journey.

In preparation for what was to come, Jake and Mike kept going over various scenarios as to what they would do, depending on what they found.

Jake regaled Mike with the latest stories he had heard from his daughters, Jennifer and Jessica, and they had each gotten some sleep.

Their adrenaline was increasing as they came closer to the beginnings of the mission, and even though neither would admit it, adventures excited them. Neither would accept failure, and they always believed they would succeed.

Since the next flight didn't leave until 10:30 in the morning, they had a light breakfast at the airport. They failed to notice two other passengers who arrived, each independently of the other. Each had met previously with their counterparts, both of whom had been on the flight from Lauderdale to Sao Paolo, and each would now continue on the flight to Buenos Aires, and each would do what they had been ordered to do: follow Jake Sullivan and Mike Lang to the ends of the earth.

CHAPTER 9

"Think I'll try to catch some shut-eye on the flight," said Mike.

"Yeah, I've noticed over the years that falling asleep for you doesn't seem to be much of a problem," said Jake.

"Comes from having a clear conscience and a good heart," replied Mike.

"Really?" he asked, to which Mike replied with only a smile.

Finally, the loudspeaker announced their flight to Buenos Aires. Mike did sleep until its arrival at Ministro Pistarini International Airport, also called Ezeiza, District 1A, due to its location in the Ezeiza Partido of Buenos Aires, about twenty-two miles south of the city.

As Samantha had previously told them, there was an Embassy staff car waiting for them with Marine Sergeant Albert Rutledge behind the wheel, who would drive them to the American Embassy at 1300 Columbia Avenue.

"How do you like the posting down here, Sergeant?" asked Jake.

"Good and bad like everywhere else, sir. Love the food. Buenos Aires is a beautiful city, but it's not home . . . you know what I mean?"

"More importantly," asked Mike, "how are things going with NCIS?"

Rutledge looked in the mirror and smiled at Mike.

"Thought maybe you wouldn't remember me Mr. Lang. It's been some time."

"Oh, I remember. That was a nice piece of work you did back in Arlington."

"FBI did all right itself," said Rutledge.

"Mike?" said Jake, looking at him quizzically.

"The good Sergeant, who really works for NCIS, the Naval Criminal Investigative Service, and I were involved in a little drug trafficking operation back in the good old days. Some young ensign got himself caught up in a mess and that got our driver involved."

"So tell me, why is NCIS driving us to the Embassy?"

"You two are probably aware that traffic of drugs, contraband, and terrorists flow south and north. It all started with another stupid, non-com getting himself involved, trying to make a few extra bucks, which got me involved. They sent me down here to find out what the hell was going on, and I've been here ever since. I've developed a rapport with a couple of the Federales, and given the high profile you two bring with you, my boss thought it might be a good idea if I enlisted their support for your transport to the Embassy."

"Things down here that bad?" asked Jake.

"Look, the contacts I've made down here are pretty good men, but we're still south of the border. Things move at their own pace . . . people tend to look the other way – perfect situation for the wrong thing to make its way through or to give advantage to some people who might not like seeing you two here."

"Any word on the street?" asked Mike.

"Nothing concrete. Same old story. Mr. Lang, always 'watch your six.'"

"Understood," said Mike.

Fortunately, the drive to the Embassy went without incident and there they were met by Simon Toliver, the Assistant to the Ambassador. Toliver directed them to the Embassy basement, where they entered a soundproof room with a desk and several chairs.

In one of the chairs sat Tomas Perez, a 52-year old Patagonian born in the town of San Antonio Oeste. Not too tall. Nothing like the "giants" of myth and legend. Thin, but wiry. Not an ounce of fat. The face was a mixture of Spanish or Portuguese with Tehuelche cheek bones and dark brown eyes. Confident but not smug. Toliver made the introductions.

"Tomas Perez, meet Jake Sullivan and Mike Lang, the gentlemen I spoke to you about."

"A pleasure," Perez said in perfect English, holding out a hand to each.

"Tomas has worked off and on for us for years. He's fluent in French, German, English, and Spanish, and has detailed knowledge of the area you're interested in. Now I'll leave you to it."

"Boy's in the CIA," said Mike.

Toliver stopped and turned around.

"You are his handler, aren't you?" asked Mike.

"Good hunting, boys," said Toliver with a smile, and exited the room.

Jake looked at Mike and said, "That went well."

"Don't worry, gentlemen," said Tomas, "he's a good man. Now, as I understand it, you two are interested in the legends of Patagonia, especially the legends of arrivals of certain persons to our shores at the end of World War II."

Jake and Mike looked at each other, not quite sure how much they should divulge.

Perez sat back in his chair.

"It's all right, gentlemen. I know you are here to hunt, though I do not know why. I have a good idea which legend you need to follow."

"And you can help us with that?" asked Mike.

"Yes, I can, Mr. Lang, and before we have further discussions, let me tell you, I don't believe it's a legend. I am almost certain that the trail you want to follow didn't end in Berlin in 1945. No, that trail followed the path of a submarine to the shores of Argentina, and then inland to the foot of the Andes at San Carlos de Bariloche . . . of that, I am certain."

CHAPTER 10

Jake's senses were on alert. He was somewhat concerned that Perez seemed to have too much knowledge about the subject of their mission.

"Tell me," Jake said, speaking to Perez, "why are you so certain . . . and why do you think that is of some concern to us?"

Perez leaned forward, placing his hands on the table.

"Mr. Lang, you are correct. Mr. Toliver is with your CIA, and he is my handler. I have worked for your government in one fashion or another for years. I was summoned here yesterday. I met with another gentleman, and he made it very clear to me that I was on special assignment and what that assignment entailed."

"And just who was this gentleman?" asked Mike.

Perez shifted in his chair and stared at Mike before answering.

"Mr. Bates, with whom I believe you two are intimately familiar."

"I'll be a son-of-a-bitch," said Mike, under his breath.

"Mr. Bates made it very clear that he was in Buenos Aires at the direction of your President Fletcher and that my sole duties and loyalties were to you and you alone . . . that the information he was going to give me was for discussion only between myself and you, and then he asked me what I thought our chances of success might be."

"Of course he did," said Jake, staring at Mike. "And what did you tell him?" asked Jake.

"I told him what I just told you. I believe we can now speak simply to each other, can we not?" and both Jake and Mike nodded. "After World War II, Adolf Hitler came to Argentina and lived here for several years. He was involved with and protected by a very powerful organization. What I do not know is where or how he came to his end, but perhaps we will find the information that allows the trail to continue. In short, gentlemen, I believe in your mission and I am at your disposal."

The Embassy provided dinner, and they stayed in the basement conference room discussing strategies, and Perez provided them information about Patagonia.

"It is a rugged land . . . sparsely populated and barren, running from the Colorado River in the north to the southern tip of South America, with coarse grasslands which caused many of the people, including my family, to become sheep farmers. We will be moving from the coast to the foothills of the Andes, the weather becoming harsher and more inclement as we travel inland. For those of us who, like myself, are born and raised there, the land has a certain beauty to it. The land rises in terraces from the Atlantic to the foot of the mountains, in some spots almost completely bare of vegetation, podded with ponds and lakes and then suddenly, as you near the foothills of the Andes, the vegetation becomes abundant with forests that rise until they meet glaciers and walls of granite. The valleys between the terraces were formed by long-ago volcanos and oncoming and retreating glacier activity, forming great depressions that run north and south, where the richest and most fertile soil exists."

Perez sat back from the table.

"What can I say gentlemen? It is my home, and perhaps its strange beauty is something only I can see."

"Your passion for your home comes through," said Mike, "and is nothing to be ashamed of, but tell me of your certainty of the existence of the man we seek in Argentina."

"I'm sure you are both familiar with all of the Nazi legends concerning what occurred at the end of the war with would-be authors, filmmakers, and simple conspiracy theorists who move from place to place, trying to prove not only the hierarchy of Nazi Germany made it safely to Argentina, but the Nazi regime still flourishes here. While there is truth to the former, I believe there is also significant truth to the latter. It seems impossible to me that, if members of the Nazi hierarchy made it to Argentina, or elsewhere, they would not somehow coordinate with each other, that there would not be some organizational structure . . . perhaps not of their making, but some other power. If Hitler escaped Germany, he had help . . . not just from his own followers, but from a more powerful source."

He sat back, lost in thought for a moment.

"I can't tell you how it all ties together. It's just a feeling I have. But we are going to the right place to begin our search. If such an organization was established, then the center of that organization was in Bariloche."

After finishing their dinner, Perez took them and showed them what he had requested – necessary clothing and supplies they would need and a change of clothes to help them assimilate into the culture of Patagonia they were about to enter. He then bid them goodnight with plans to continue their final preparations in the morning, and then leave for their 2:30 flight that afternoon.

After Perez departed, they again were met by Toliver, who took them to the armory and supplied them with the weaponry they selected, and also, diplomatic credentials to allow them to carry their weapons while in Argentina.

Jake and Mike spent the rest of the evening going over the maps Perez had provided them, doing their own check of their supplies and weapons, and then heading for bed, anxious for the adventure to begin.

CHAPTER 11

Sergeant Rutledge again transported them, along with Tomas Perez, to the airport for their 2:30 flight to San Carlos de Bariloche.

The flight itself was uneventful, most of the scenery obscured by thick cloud cover that had moved in from the Atlantic. They arrived on time, at approximately 5:00 P.M.

Jake, Mike, and Perez got a cab, which took them to their rooms at the Tirol in Bariloche. As they drove through the town square, Mike looked out in amazement.

"This place looks like something out of Bavaria . . . snow-capped mountains . . . alpine architecture."

"It is all by design, Mr. Lang," Perez said. "This was a small village on the southern shore of Lake Nahuel Huapi that gradually, over the years, had an influx of German settlers. In the 1930s and 1940s, there were extensive public works done, replicating the alpine style of architecture from their homeland . . . that, and the Nazi legends of which we spoke, has caused it to become a major tourism center with skiing, trekking, and mountaineering facilities, with numerous restaurants, cafes, and chocolate shops."

"So, what you're saying, Tomas," said Jake, "is even here the undercurrent of evil seems to go hand in hand with the beauty around it?"

"I'm afraid so," said Tomas. "It is the way of the world, is it not?"

Jake nodded in agreement.

"Unfortunately so."

After they had checked in, Jake, Mike and Tomas met in the hotel lobby. As they stepped outside, a Range Rover pulled up and a man got out and handed Tomas the keys.

"I've arranged a vehicle we will need to travel where I believe the trail will lead us, and now I must go meet someone who can provide us important information."

"You're going alone?" asked Mike.

"I'm sorry, but I must. This contact is afraid, very afraid. I have known him for years, and I believe he trusts me. I must use that trust to get him to talk to all of us. I hope to be back in a few hours."

Mike looked at Jake.

"Go ahead, Tomas. Do what you need to do. We'll wait here. And do your best . . . it sounds like we need this man."

"I always do my best, Mr. Sullivan . . . always," and with that, he got in the vehicle and drove away.

CHAPTER 12

Tomas was true to his word and two hours later he was back, where he found Jake and Mike seated over coffee in the hotel lounge.

"Success?" asked Mike.

"Indeed," said Tomas, as the waitress came over. "The same please," he said, pointing to the cups in front of Mike and Jake. "The man is ten miles toward the mountains and works on a ranch there. He had an uncle who witnessed the submarine landing at the Gulf of San Matías in 1945. According to this man, his uncle went to the United States because he felt he had an obligation to report the things he had seen and what he knew, and then the uncle simply disappeared. He has agreed to meet with us tomorrow and to tell us what he knows."

"Excellent," said Jake. "So, now all we have to do is wait."

"There is a fine restaurant here where I have eaten before, the Naan Restaurant. It's in the Belgrano residential district and over-looks the city and the lake . . . a beautiful view. I suggest we have a late dinner, my treat," looking at his watch, knowing it was already 8:00 o'clock.

"I agree," said Jake, "and we thank you, Tomas."

"Well," said Tomas, "I need a shower and a change of clothes. Shall we meet in one-half hour?"

With their plans made, all three headed toward the elevator to make ready. As soon as they departed, a man who had been sitting on the farthest side of the lounge away from them, folded his newspaper, headed outside, and entered a parked vehicle driven by a man who had been on the flight from Buenos Aires to Bariloche. One of the men took a cell phone from his pocket and made a call as they sat there waiting for events to unfold.

CHAPTER 13

Tomas had been right. The restaurant had a beautiful view overlooking the city and the lake, with lights along the shoreline reflecting in the still waters. The snow-capped mountains overlooking the alpine village made it seem like they were looking through a snow globe.

They were busy talking about Tomas's childhood in Patagonia when a man and woman came in and sat down to dine. Mike was sure that he had seen the man before on one of their flights and nudged Jake and nodded in their direction. Jake had the same thought, and decided to find out.

"I'm sorry to intrude. My name is Jake Sullivan, and I'm almost certain we've met before."

Jake took the man in. He was young, tall, and muscular. His eyes seemed to move around the room, taking everything in, not missing anything. His wife was attractive, and she also seemed physically fit, exuding a strength and a confidence that was hard to mistake.

"It's a pleasure to meet you, Mr. Sullivan, but I'm afraid you have me confused with someone else. I don't think I've ever had the pleasure. Janie, have you ever met Mr. Sullivan?"

"I don't believe I have," she said in a southern drawl, "and I apologize for my husband, Mr. Sullivan, we are Samuel and Janie

Russell of Atlanta, Georgia. My husband Samuel is one of the current owners of Russell Stover Confections."

"A pleasure, Mrs. Russell, and I apologize. I simply thought you were someone else," and he turned to walk away. "Oh," said Jake, turning back, "do you have a business card I could have, Mr. Russell?"

"Absolutely," he said, pulling one from his pocket and handing it to Jake.

"I don't mean to be intrusive," said Jake, "but what brings you to a place like this?"

"Chocolate," said Samuel Russell. "We're trying to make some in-roads into the chocolate market here. Sales figures coming out of this place are amazing."

"Of course," said Jake. "Again, my apologies. Enjoy your dinner."

Jake smiled and walked away and went back to his table. He put the card on the table between he and Mike. They paid no further attention to the couple.

Jake, Mike, and Tomas had just finished their dinner and were getting ready to leave when Samuel Russell and his wife Janie came to their table.

"I have to apologize, Mr. Sullivan. My wife Janie is much more up on current events than I am, and she explained to me who you were . . . and she also recognized whom I believe is Mike Lang," he said, extending his hand.

"I am," said Mike, standing and shaking hands, "and this is our friend, Tomas Perez."

"A pleasure, Mr. Perez," said Mr. Russell, nodding.

Janie Russell went on, "I've read so much about you two. I can't believe I'm actually getting to meet you."

As always, Jake's response was the same.

"Please, don't believe everything you read."

"You two have done so much for our great country. We're just honored to meet you."

"Thank you very much," said Jake and Mike.

"Well, we'll let you be," said Janie, and they exited.

"See the way that guy moves?" said Mike. "And her, too . . . candy salesman my ass."

As Samuel and Janie Russell walked along together, Samuel spoke into a microphone hidden under his cuff on his right sleeve.

"I'm pretty sure they made us. Send in the next team."

The two men observing the Russells leave did not overhear the conversation.

CHAPTER 14

When Jake got back to his room, it had been tossed and searched completely. An envelope had been slipped under the door with a note inside that said:

Meet me tomorrow morning at 10:00 A.M., at Refugio Otto Meiling. I have your answers.

Jake alerted Mike and they walked down the hall and rapped on Tomas's door. He answered in pajamas, obviously ready for bed.

"What is it? I was just getting ready for bed."

"Our room has been tossed," said Jake, "and this note was under the door. What's it mean?"

"It's one of the huts established by the Club Andino. They set up these huts along all the hiking trails in the area. This one is right beside a glacier. It shouldn't be too busy this time of year. This guy's a local by the choice he made – it's a good spot. We have to go out to Pampa Linda, about 30 miles outside the city, to start our trek up the mountain. The hut's perched right on the edge of the Castano Overa Glacier. Tourist buses run out there daily, but not this time of year. We can head up to the mountain first thing in the morning."

"What time is our meeting with your contact?"

"He wanted to put in a full day's work at the ranch and get his day's wages, so not until 5:00 o'clock at the local bar."

"So, we have time?" asked Mike.

"Yes, we can do it."

Tomas had an odd look on his face.

"Do you think it's a trap?"

"It's possible," said Tomas, "but I guess we have to find out. From now on, we travel armed. You are still armed, I presume?"

Mike reached to his back and withdrew his Glock from his holster.

"Always am, my friend . . . always am. How high are we going?" asked Mike.

"About a thousand meters. How are your legs?"

Jake looked at Mike.

"I guess we're going to find out."

CHAPTER 15

Jake and Mike arose early in the morning, about 6:00 A.M., showered and dressed, and knocked on Tomas's door, but he didn't answer. They went downstairs. Fortunately, the café was open, and they ordered coffee and rolls.

It was not long before Tomas came in the door, also dressed and ready to go.

"I was talking to some people I know in the street, as well as people who work here. Whoever tossed your room were professionals. No one saw anyone, coming or leaving. I suggest we be very careful on this trip. I have the Range Rover out front whenever you're ready."

Downing the last of his coffee, Jake looked at Mike.

"Ready?"

"As I'll ever be," said Mike, picking up a roll to take with him, and they headed out the door.

CHAPTER 16

Tomas was right. The air gradually got colder as the three men made their way up the mountain slope, at first encountering a soft grade, heavily forested with just a beaten path to follow, until they finally rose above the tree line to a more barren landscape that gave way to a craggy, rocky summit with a brick hut sitting on top. They were bent low, using their hands as well as their feet, to make their way to the summit when a rock spray erupted at Mike's feet.

"Get down!" he shouted. "Shots fired!" and all three men went prone on the rocky surface.

Jake and Mike both drew their weapons and Mike rolled to his right, moving away from the space he had occupied. Jake did the same, to his left, so he was almost touching Tomas. They looked at each other and nodded, both rising up and firing in the direction from where the shots had come, on the right-hand side of the stone hut. They saw two figures approaching, each carrying silenced, automatic weapons. Right before they went prone and the area around them again erupted with broken rock, Mike raised his arm and fired in the general direction that he believed their attackers were moving, and Jake did the same.

Finally, the guns went silent, and after several seconds, Mike and Jake each rose so they could see the terrain in front of them and saw two bodies, no more than a hundred yards away.

CHAPTER 17

As Jake, Mike, and Tomas approached, they were cautious even though there was no movement from the two men lying in front of them. They were clad all in black, wearing bullet proof vests and ski masks.

Kicking their weapons away, Mike checked one while Jake checked the other, but found no pulse. One man had died of a head shot and the other had been hit in the neck.

"Who the hell are these guys?" said Mike.

"Give me a hand. I think there's a way we can find out," said Jake, as he began removing the gloves from the attacker nearest him and rolling up his sleeves. Mike, understanding what he was doing, began the same exercise with the attacker nearest him and found what they were looking for.

"Here it is," said Mike, holding up the man's forearm, the inside of which had the Group 45 tattoo. "How long do you think they've been on to us?" asked Mike.

"Probably since we started," said Jake, shaking his head and rising, looking at the hut, then back at the dead men, and then back in the direction from whence they had come. "Mike, let me ask you a question. How did you think these two guys were going to come down that slope after us?"

"I figured they were going to try to flank us."

"So did I," said Jake, "and I placed my shots accordingly."

"Me, too," said Mike.

"Then how the hell did we hit these guys? Such perfect shots . . . one in the head and one in the neck . . . they were coming down the center together."

"Dumb luck?" asked Mike.

"Perhaps they were further apart," said Tomas, "and converged by staggering to this place after they were hit."

"I guess it's possible, but something seems off."

"I'm going to go check the hut," said Tomas.

"Go ahead," said Mike, "but be careful. I guarantee you there's no one waiting to meet us . . . it was a trap the whole way."

Tomas climbed to the top, carefully looked in one of the windows of the hut, and looked back down at them and shook his head, indicating there was no one present, and then started on his way back.

"Nothing, right?" said Mike.

"So how do we play it from here on out?" asked Tomas.

"Nothing goes beyond we three," said Jake, looking at Tomas, "and I mean nothing. We discuss all our plans outside, and we challenge anyone who looks suspicious. Tomas, can you get word to your friend we are supposed to meet later today?"

"I can," said Tomas.

"Make up a story. Pick a new location that only you know, that hopefully, he won't talk about."

"Don't worry. He's scared to death. He's not going to say anything."

"Good. Let's keep it that way," said Mike. "Hopefully, he can give us some information that will keep us one step ahead of everybody else. Now, let's get the hell off this mountain!" And they headed down.

CHAPTER 18

Late that afternoon Tomas found Jake and Mike sitting on the patio, deep in discussion.

"How's things with your friend?" asked Jake, as Tomas approached. Tomas shook his head.

"He changed the location. He's too scared. He doesn't want to leave the ranch. He swore to me that he saw some men moving through the forest near the hacienda, and he's afraid someone else knows of the information he has."

"Why does he feel so safe at this place, Tomas?" asked Mike.

"The Incalco Ranch . . . it's on the shore of Lake Nahuel Huapi, about 80 kilometers north of here. Supposedly this is where the Nazi party in Argentina stashed Hitler, Eva Braun, and their child. The place belonged to a wealthy businessman named Antonio, who was one of Perón's most trusted friends. It sits amid a pine forest and you can only reach it by boat or hydroplane, and there are guards all over the place."

"And that's why he feels safe," said Jake.

"Exactly," said Tomas, "with the guards and the other workers there, he feels he has a better chance than coming out in the open."

"So how do we get to him?" Mike asked.

"Anyone expecting us to come in would expect us to come by water . . . a plane is too noisy . . . but there are paths through the forest. They are tough, but they're there, and I know where they are. I can almost guarantee we can get in without being noticed . . . if there is anyone watching."

"Your friend, Tomas, what's his name?"

"Diego Cruz."

"This Diego Cruz is the only lead we have. Someone out there is trying to get to him and get the same information," said Jake.

"Trying to get the information is bad enough, but if they're just taking a wild guess, they might be more eager to get him. Their best option is to silence him. Either way, we have to get out there," said Mike.

Tomas nodded in agreement.

"We'll leave in an hour. Dress carefully. We're going through heavy woods in the dark."

"Tomas, it's not that I don't trust you," said Mike, "but how the hell are you going to find this place?"

"Don't forget, Mr. Lang, I grew up in this area. The tourists have been coming here a long time, many of whom are deeply involved in Hitler myth and wanted to see one of the places where he supposedly stayed in Argentina. The owners of the facility try to discourage these things as much as possible, but if you had been a young man, such as Diego or me, for a few dollars, you discover ways to get people in close without alerting the residents."

"A man of many talents, Tomas," said Mike.

"We shall see, Mr. Lang. We shall see."

CHAPTER 19

Tomas had driven in on a dirt track under cover of the woods, but close enough that they could see the moonlight reflecting on the lake.

They got out, checked their gear and weapons, and studied the lights across the lake.

"How far away is that?" asked Jake.

"About a mile and a half," answered Tomas.

Just then, Tomas's cell phone buzzed.

"Calm down, Diego . . . calm down. I'm here now. All right . . . we'll meet you. We're starting in. Yes . . . yes . . . be careful."

"What is it?" asked Jake.

"It's Diego. He kept saying, 'They're here. They've come to get me. They're here.' He's taking the path from the house at the ranch, toward us. We have to move," and with that, Tomas started, walking briskly ahead. "Keep up," he said, looking back.

"Let's go," said Jake to Mike. "That wasn't a request, that was an order," and they both hurried to catch up.

CHAPTER 20

The path had widened out and became somewhat flat, and they once again could see the moonlight on the lake, with the lights of the hacienda shining brighter and closer.

"No! No!"

Just then, they saw Tomas go down on one knee beside something lying on the ground mingled with the pinecones and moss on the forest floor.

"No, no," he said again, softly, his words being carried away in the wind that rustled the trees above them. And then, he stood up and turned away.

"It's Diego. He's dead. Shot twice in the back."

Mike knelt down beside the body.

"They must have used silencers. Tomas, I'm sorry, but I have to move him."

Tomas remained facing away and just shook his head in the affirmative. Mike rolled the body over and could see that his jacket pockets and pants pockets had been searched and then he felt something on the ground. It was partially wet and sticky. Diego's blood. He pulled it out of the dirt and shook it.

"Tomas, did Diego wear a cap?"

Tomas turned and looked.

"Yes, that's it."

Mike looked at the scene and kept looking at the hat in his hand.

"What is it, Mike?" asked Jake.

"Could be just the way they moved the body, but why would his cap be directly underneath him? I mean, if he was shot from behind and he lurched forward, the cap could have flown off anywhere, or it could have stayed on. How would it get right beneath his body?"

"Let me take a look at it," said Jake, and he felt the cap, inside and out. "Wait a minute . . . there's something in here. Tomas, do you have your knife?"

Both Tomas and Mike moved toward Jake, and Tomas handed over his knife that Jake used to cut open the cap and pull out a small piece of paper.

"It's too dark," said Jake, "I can't make out what it says."

Tomas said, "Unzip your jacket and hold it close to your chest. Mr. Lang, move over here," and with that, Tomas brought out a small penlight and shown it on the piece of paper, which said:

Left top bedpost – bunk.

"We must move. Now, come, gentlemen . . . I have a plan," said Tomas. And with that, he opened his coat to reveal an Army 45 in a holster on his right hip, which he took out and fired twice into the air. "We need to get going. It won't take them long to get here."

"What the hell are you doing, Tomas?" said Mike.

"As I said, I have a plan. I know what the note means. I'll explain as we go." And he did.

CHAPTER 21

Jake and Mike were parked in a gravel lot beside a small dock on the other side of the lake, as they watched a small boat carrying Tomas move across its surface. They had been there for several hours. Tomas insisted they wait until Diego's body was found and activity began at the dock. Tomas was obviously well known in the area and spoke freely with the police when they showed up, as well as those that had crossed the lake from the hacienda, and his pleas to go see his friend received approval.

"So, Tomas thinks that whatever Diego wanted to share with us is in a bedpost at the bunkhouse at the hacienda . . . is that the plan?" asked Mike.

"It is," said Jake.

"And if it isn't?"

"Then we're back to square one."

"I just realized something. You and I haven't been on a stakeout."

"This isn't exactly a stakeout."

"It's close. We're in a car . . . it's dark . . . waiting for something to happen."

"That's it? That's what you've got?"

Mike just looked at him and said, "I think I'll get some sleep."

"Again, as usual."

He closed his eyes and was soon fast asleep, with Jake just smiling to himself and shaking his head.

CHAPTER 22

It was not necessary for Tomas to pretend grief and guilt as he stood over the body of his friend. Those feelings were genuine, as was the anger that was rising inside him to obtain justice for Diego Cruz, and he made a silent vow to himself that those who did this would pay.

After he paid his respects, he turned and approached the police officer who was obviously in charge.

"Thank you, Captain Esteban. I appreciate you allowing me to come."

"I know you and Diego were close, and I'm sorry for your loss."

"Where did you find him?"

"People here indicate shots rang out on the west side of the lake on one of the paths and workers found him lying there."

"Who would have done such a thing?"

"There's very little evidence . . . at least what we can see right now. We'll come back in the daylight and see what we can find."

"I truly hope you get them, Captain."

"I promise you, Tomas, we'll do our best."

"I'm going to head back to the dock and wait for a boat going home. Thank you again."

"Certainly, Tomas, certainly."

Tomas headed back away from the main house where they were keeping Diego's body, heading in the general direction of the dock. As soon as he was sure no one was watching, he slipped into the shadows to his left and by a round-a-bout way, he took a path to the back of the bunkhouse where the hacienda workers stayed. As he suspected, there was no one there, as he looked through one of the windows. All the staff were agitated and upset about Diego and the fact that killers had come into their midst. He was sure that a few felt shame and guilt because they had not taken Diego's claim about the threat seriously.

Slowly, he made his way around to the front. Crouching low, he made his way along the porch to the door and opened it and entered.

He had been here before visiting Diego on many occasions and knew where his bunk was and made his way directly to it. Heading to the top left bedpost, which helped form a frame made out of rough wood and slabs of timber, he moved his hand along it and found the cut he was looking for along the top. Taking out his knife, he inserted it in the cut and began to pry. Soon the wooden top came off. He could only put two fingers inside but felt paper that had been rolled and put in the hole. Using the two fingers, he kept edging the paper to the surface until finally, it came free, and he saw that he was holding five or six envelopes bundled together, when he heard footsteps on the porch and the door opening.

Pushing the top back on, folding his knife and putting it in his pocket, and shoving the envelopes in his jacket as he sat down on the bunk, were done in one quick fluid motion, when the door opened and the lights were turned on. And there stood Captain Esteban and several of his men.

Esteban had been a police officer for a long time. Tomas knew he was going to have to dispel what Esteban would surely believe was a suspicious situation.

"Tomas, what are you doing here? I thought you were leaving."

"I was, Captain, but," he said, looking around, "my guilt overcame me."

"What guilt, Tomas?"

"Several days ago, we had met and talked. He told me he had seen men out in the pines. For some reason he thought they were after him. I asked him why and he wouldn't say. You know Diego. I thought he was making something out of nothing." He could see Esteban relaxing.

"We've heard the same story from people here, Tomas. Why are you here?"

"I don't know. We used to sit here, like this, and talk. I was on my way to the dock and . . . I don't know . . . I just wanted to sit here one more time. I just feel like I could have done something."

Esteban walked over and looked down at Tomas and stared at him for a while. Finally, he put his hand on his shoulder.

"Tomas, whatever happened, it's not your fault. You can't blame yourself."

"I wish I could believe that, Captain. I don't know if I can," and he got up. "I'm sorry for coming here if it's a problem."

"No, it's all right, Tomas. It's all right. We just need to check Diego's things and see if he left anything that might give us some hint as to what was going on here."

"I understand," said Tomas, looking around. "All these years . . . he didn't have much, did he?"

"No," said Esteban, also scanning the area of Diego's bed. "I don't think we're going to find anything here that's going to be helpful, but we have to uncover every stone."

"Would you keep me posted if you get any news, Captain?"

"I will, Tomas, I will. I think there is a boat that is ready to leave. You should hurry to the dock."

"I'm on my way, Captain. Again, thank you," and with that, he headed out the door.

CHAPTER 23

Jake poked Mike awake as Tomas got off the boat and walked into the gravel lot toward their vehicle.

"He's back," said Jake.

"What time is it?" asked Mike.

"Don't worry . . . you got your one hour beauty sleep."

"Feels like I could use a whole lot more," said Mike, stretching in every direction and yawning at the same time.

Tomas quickly opened the door and entered the back seat. Jake and Mike turned half around. Tomas held up the rolled packet of envelopes. When Jake and Mike saw it, they nodded. Then Jake started the car and they headed back to Bariloche.

CHAPTER 24

As they entered the hotel, Tomas turned.

"I don't know about you two, but I feel terrible. It's already 4:00 A.M., and I have a feeling we're going to be spending the rest of the night going over these," as he held up the bundle of envelopes. "I, for one, am going to get a hot shower and order some coffee and rolls. Where shall we meet?"

"Sounds like an excellent idea, Tomas," said Jake, and he motioned for everybody to move closer. "Where's the best place around here at this hour of the night that probably wouldn't be bugged by anybody interested in us?"

Tomas said, "Come to my room in one hour."

CHAPTER 25

At almost 5:00 A.M., on the nose, Jake and Mike rapped on Tomas's door, and he opened it, ushering them in. He had ordered coffee and rolls from room service and the smell and the warmth filled the room.

"We can talk freely here, gentlemen," he said, as he closed the door and motioned them toward the food and drink.

Jake and Mike both poured themselves a cup of coffee and took a roll and sat in one of the chairs Tomas had placed around the bed, on which were four envelopes, each with one sheet of paper attached.

"Tomas, how long have you been more than just an asset of the C.I.A.?", asked Mike, causing Jake to stop in mid drink, and Tomas to stand very still, staring at him.

"C'mon, Tomas . . . what you did tonight . . . the way you took over that situation . . . you've obviously swept this room to know that it's safe to talk here. You've got some pretty unique skills . . . valuable to only a few agencies in the world. Given your notoriety in our Embassy, I'm sort of thinking you have a history."

Tomas sighed and sat down.

"I was a young man when the British went to war with us over the Falkland Islands. I was recruited into the 602 Commando Company in May of 1982. I was young. War is always glamorous until you fight in one. We fought several battles with our British counterparts, and we were trained by the best of many nations after the war ended. My missions were many until I left. I had enough of killing."

"Hey, I have no problem with it," said Mike, "I'm just glad you're one of the good guys . . . at least I think."

Even Tomas had to chuckle.

"I understand your hesitation. Sometimes, given what I have been asked to do, I wonder myself about the relative definition of good and bad."

"Well," said Jake, clearing his throat, "that's out of the way. Now, what about this paperwork?"

"I've already read them. The dates start on your left and move to your right. These are letters from Alfonso Duarté, Diego Cruz's uncle. Please, take your time," he said, as Jake and Mike began to read each one. The first letter, dated June 2, 1945, read as follows:

" *My dearest Helena, I am sorry I had to leave without giving you any advance notice, but I can no longer live with the secrets that I possess. I am crossing the mountains to the coast and have found passage on a ship that will ultimately take me to Los Angeles, California, United States. There I hope to meet with someone from the government so that I may unburden my soul. You will remember last month when I and a few others were hired in mid-May to do some work near the Gulf of San Matas, but I never told you what that work entailed. I never told you what was involved that night, and will not now, as I do not wish to burden you as I have been burdened since that time. Two submarines came to shore – one to make sure everything was safe, and a second to drop off passengers. Evil came to Argentina that night. Evil in the form of a man and a woman and hangers-on, loaded onto pack horses and moved inland, toward the foothills of the southern Andes. I must do this, my dearest wife, so that my conscience will be clear, and that our country might be rid of this evil, and those who have facilitated it being here. I will write again. – Alfonso"*

The second letter was dated June 10th:

"I have arrived in Los Angeles and have begun a conversation with a reporter from The Los Angeles Examiner. If he proves trustworthy, I hope to ultimately meet with him and give him the necessary information. He may turn it over to government authorities and our lives returned to normal. I believe the evil I spoke of is being aided by high government officials of Argentina, and I think it might be best that we begin a new life here in the United States. If such a decision becomes necessary, I hope that you will agree to come and be with me so that we may start a new life in a new world. I will write again. -- Alfonso"

The third letter was dated July 27th:

"The person I wrote of in my previous letter is only a friend of the reporter I seek to con de in, and they have agreed to a meeting with me tomorrow, and, hopefully, this burden will be lifted from me and all will be well. I think of you often and hope you are well, and that we will be together soon. – Alfonso"

The last letter was dated July 30, 1945:

"I met the reporter and found him to be trustworthy and gave him the details of that night in May. I explained how the two submarines appeared and how approximately fty people in all were of oaded, and who I was able to recognize, and how they were taken inland by three men through the auspices of six Argentine of - cials. I worry now that it is done whether or not I am safe, and I must tell you that in our secret hiding place is $15,000.00 that I was paid to help in this matter. You can use it to come to me when you next hear from me. Be careful who you speak to and what you do. I have given them the name of a man at a hotel in San Antonio who can take them to the ranch where evil dwells. If you do not hear from me again, I am sorry that I caused you such grief and despair, but this was something I had to do. I only hope that my new friend, 'Jack' was honest with me. – Alfonso"

CHAPTER 26

They had finished reading the letters when Mike spoke up.

"All right, we assume the 'evil' Alfonso wrote of to his wife was Hitler. All this does, Jake, is reinforce your theory that he escaped Germany and came here. It doesn't tell us what he did, who he was, nothing."

"I know," said Jake, throwing the last letter on the bed. "It doesn't give us any idea whatsoever."

"I'm sorry," said Tomas. "Perhaps Diego could have given us more," and his voice dropped.

Jake got up and started walking around the room.

"Let's think, and see what we have. Alfonso was never heard from again, so let's assume that whatever he told this reporter got him killed. If that's the case, Hitler would not have had to leave Argentina, so what did he do with his life?"

"Yeah, but if you're right," said Mike, "he spent a lot of his time working for Group 45."

"Yeah, but he would have had to have some kind of cover . . . some legitimate business interest, or something."

"Or . . ." said Tomas, "he could have simply stayed at the hacienda and gave his directives, using the various Nazi networks to do his bidding."

"Wait a minute," said Jake, as he pulled out his phone. "What was it Walsh told us when he was going over Simon's ramblings?" moving his fingers rapidly over his phone. "Here it is. He came across a painting that matched some of the words Simon used. The painting was called 'The Old Building In Stand Of Trees'. Painting . . . that was Hitler's true passion. That's what he always wanted to do, but he was never good enough," said Jake, thinking to himself, but speaking aloud as he walked around the room. "Tomas, is there any way we can check the town records to see if there were any art galleries here . . . that started a short time after 1945?"

"I can do better than that," said Tomas.

CHAPTER 27

"There is only one gallery of any significance, and that is the Klibing Gallery, which has been here for years," said Tomas, looking at his watch. "It's 6:00 A.M., and it doesn't open until 9:00. State your preference, gentlemen . . . a little nap, or breakfast?"

"I don't know about sleeping beauty, here," said Jake, "but I'm awake. A good breakfast would be just fine."

"Very funny," said Mike. "I had my nap. I'm ready to go."

"Then let's be on our way," said Tomas. "There's a great little place off of one of the side streets that specializes in breakfasts like you can get in an American diner . . . and it opens at 6:00."

"Sounds like my kind of place," said Mike, as they headed out the door.

CHAPTER 28

They all agreed breakfast had been wonderful. Fried eggs, hash browns, sausage, toast, and lots of coffee. Feeling reinvigorated, they headed toward the main square of Bariloche, where Tomas found a parking spot and led the rest of the way on foot, hoping to find the owner there before opening.

"It still feels like I'm back in Bavaria," said Mike, as he walked.

"That's what it's supposed to do," said Jake. "That's why it's such an attraction."

"It gives me the creeps," said Mike.

"Here we are," said Tomas, as he stopped in front of a doorway to a small storefront, with a sign that read: 'Klibing Gallery – Fine Paintings – Established 1954'.

As they entered, a small bell tinkled and an older man, glasses low on his nose, looked up from a counter where he had been reviewing some paperwork.

"Good morning, gentlemen," he said. "How can I be of assistance to you?"

"Are you the owner?" asked Jake.

"I am . . . Hans Klibing."

Jake extended his hand and said, "Pleased to meet you, sir. My name is Jake Sullivan, and this is my associate, Mike Lang, and our local reference, Tomas Perez."

"A pleasure, gentlemen," said Klibing, looking over the three of them.

"We've been employed by a documentary film company to do a little research and ground work here in your lovely town. This is such a gem that not enough people are aware of. The producers, who work for a world travel concern, are interested in making a major documentary to show off the beauty of this particular area of the world. In doing our research, we saw that your gallery was established in 1954 and, therefore, you've been here for quite some time, and I was wondering if we could ask you a few questions?"

The owner of the Klibing Gallery was already calculating how he could turn this to his advantage and make himself the center of such a documentary, thereby drawing more and more people to his shop when they came to the beautiful town of Bariloche.

"Why, yes . . . I'm not particularly busy at the moment," he said, shuffling the papers on the counter and pushing them to the side, "so long as it doesn't take too long. You know, my customers will start coming in shortly, but I do have some time."

Mike picked up the charade.

"This is a beautiful shop you have. Ahh . . . what was it before?"

"I purchased it as an ongoing gallery."

"That's interesting," said Mike. "Could you give us some of the details?"

"Yes, yes. Actually, the shop was much bigger. It comprised the buildings on both sides of this one. Herr Stephan Gunselman, who ran the Gunselman Studio, had a much larger business than I do. He was involved in importing and exporting on the international art market and used both of the additional spaces as warehouses."

Mike continued, taking notes as he went, "And when did Mr. Gunselman begin the gallery . . . if you know?"

"Oh, sometime in the late 1940s . . . 46 perhaps . . . 47 . . . something like that."

Jake, who had also taken out a notebook and a pen was now writing.

"And who ran the business with Mr. Gunselman?"

"By the time I bought it, I know his wife had died, and I believe he had one son . . . ummm . . . I think he was around fourteen or fifteen when I purchased the business," said Herr Klibing, looking into space, searching for something. "Alios," he said, "Alios . . . that was the boy's name. I remember it now. I don't think he had any other people involved in the gallery, except for people who would work the warehouses for him, except for . . . what was his name?"

"Who's that?" asked Mike.

"There was an American who came to visit quite often . . . I'm trying to think . . . I can't place it now."

"What did he look like?" asked Jake.

Klibing finally became wary.

"Why are you asking so many questions about the former owners? I thought this was to be a documentary about the town as it is now?"

"Oh, you know these people," said Mike, "all they care about is background. We take all this time, do all this work, give them all this information, and then they never use it."

"Ahhh, yes," Klibing said, smiling. "I understand what you mean."

"Ahhh, the American?" again prodded Jake.

"What he looked like? Well dressed. Always wore a suit, wire-rimmed glasses, average height and build . . . Trent! That was his name!"

"Well," said Jake, looking at Mike, "I think that's enough information about old history. Let's now talk about you and your shop. How did the sale come about? When did you take over? How did you consolidate into just this one storefront?"

"It was a funny thing the way it happened," said Hans. "I owned a very, very small shop . . . just dealing with local artists . . . and one day, in walked Mr. Gunselman, and he told me that some urgent business was taking he and his son away, back to Europe, I believe he said, and that he wanted to sell me his business. I explained to him that I had no interest in the importing or exporting business, and he asked me what if he could sell the two warehouse parcels separately and sell me the store front to expand my shop. I again explained that I probably didn't have sufficient funds to make such a purchase, and he told me not to worry . . . that he would work out a deal because he always liked me and he had to leave, and he did. The terms were very favorable. He practically gave the place away."

"And did he go back to Europe? And by going back, I presume you mean he was from Europe?"

"Yes, he wasn't from here originally. He had come from Europe like so many did at the end of the war."

"So how long did the transaction take?" asked Jake.

"Oh, it was over very quickly. Only a few days after I spoke with him, he had everything ready. I signed the paperwork. He gave me the key . . . and the next day, he was gone. It was as if he had not been here."

"Well, thank you," said Jake. "We appreciate your time. You've been very helpful, and we'll be back for another session."

"Well, I would hope so, so I can tell you something about my shop."

"Exactly," said Mike. "We have to submit this segment on the past history, and the next segment will be on the present owner, which, of course, will feature you."

This brought a smile to Hans's face, as he thought about being a star of a documentary.

"Very good, gentlemen. Don't hesitate to call upon me anytime."

"Once again, we thank you for your time," said Jake, and they exited the premises.

Standing on the sidewalk, Jake was studying his notepad.

"What's your gut telling you?" asked Mike.

"That I know who Stephan Gunselman really was, and we need to find where he went."

CHAPTER 29

"Sam, this is Jake Sullivan. I'm sorry, but I have another priority request."

"I've been told to put you at the top of the list, Mr. Sullivan. What do you need?"

"I need you to check on the name Trent. We think it might have been an alias used by Judge Branson. Also, on an art dealer that was in Bariloche from 1945 to 1954, named Stephan Gunselman. Had a son named Alios. Don't know the spelling. We're trying to find out where they might have gone to. They were in the importing and exporting business of international art."

"You think this could be our friend?"

"It's a possibility . . . certainly the best lead we have right now."

"I'm on it. I'll get back to you as soon as I can."

"Thanks, Sam," and the line went dead.

Jake turned to Mike and Tomas, who had been listening to the call.

"Did I leave anything out?"

"Nope, I think you got it," said Mike.

"Let's go back to the hotel and wait . . . give Sam some time to work his magic. If he doesn't come up with anything, we head home."

"Great," said Mike, "more time in Little Bavaria."

"Don't worry, Mr. Lang," said Tomas, "you spend enough time here, it might grow on you."

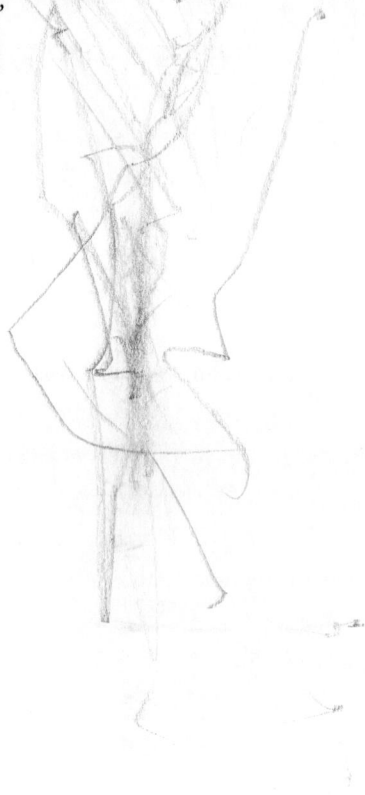

CHAPTER 30

Forty-eight hours came and went with no word from Sam Walsh. Jake would make inquiries every couple of hours, but nothing was turning up. Jake called Jason Bates to report their progress, and Bates, as always, was upset at how little progress had been made.

"A week in South America?" asked Bates. "And this is all you've come up with?"

"Doing the best we can with what we have, Jason. Hopefully, Sam Walsh can take the information we gave him and give us another lead to follow."

"I sure as hell hope so!" shouted Bates. "Group 45's activities are increasing everywhere . . . and without that key, we have no idea who or what we're dealing with. I sure as hell hope your gut wasn't wrong this time, Jake."

"I'll let you know," said Jake. "We're going to give it another twenty-four hours, Jason. Get us flights home from here the day after tomorrow. If we don't hear anything by then, we'll come back and brief the President in person and go from there."

"Hope Walsh can give you something, Jake. Otherwise, it won't be a pretty experience," and Bates hung up the phone.

Mike, who had been laying stretched out on the bed flipping through a local magazine, looked up.

"Sounds like the usual Jason."

"You got that right," said Jake.

CHAPTER 31

It was at 2:00 A.M., the following morning that Jake's phone rang. Jake, still dressed and sprawled across the bed, checked caller I.D. and was immediately wide awake.

"It's 2:00 o'clock in the morning, Sam. I know you have something."

"That, I do. Look, I'm putting a lot of different stuff together here, but I've got a hunch it's going to take you where you need to go."

"I'm going to put you on speaker so Mike can hear this, too, as soon as he's awake."

Mike, who had fallen asleep in a chair in Jake's room, responded, "I'm awake, I'm awake. Go ahead, Sam."

"Okay, first thing . . . I think you were right about our good friend, Judge Edmund C. Branson, visiting our boy in Argentina. Going over those records you found at the mansion . . . he talked about traveling south right after 1945."

"Doesn't necessarily mean Argentina," said Mike.

"No, but the funny thing about those trips . . . they ended after 1954."

"When Gunselman sold the business," said Jake.

"Exactly," said Walsh. "And one other thing. Guess what Judge Branson's grandfather's name was?"

Mike looked up. "Trent?"

"Bingo."

"Nice work," said Jake. "Tell me you have more."

"I do. I couldn't find a single thing on Gunselman. That turned out to be a complete dead end, but when I did a wider search on South American art galleries, I found out that a museum, gallery, and education center called 'The Metro' was built in Tampico, Mexico."

"And what's the connection?" asked Jake.

"Something called 'The Judge Edmund C. Branson Foundation' donated $250,000.00 while it was being built. And something else I found when checking art galleries . . . there was one major importer and exporter in Tampico of international art, which just happened to start in 1954 . . . someone named Strausser. Also, I listened to the recording of Branson made by Commander Donahower after he had been shot in Paris. I think you boys need to get to Tampico, Mexico . . . pronto. I'll keep looking."

And with that, he was gone.

CHAPTER 32

Jake reached for his phone and brought up the recording of Simon's last words. He and Mike heard at the same time, "Metro. House with trees," and then the sound "meh."

"Metro. Hitler's painting. And maybe he was starting to say Mexico," said Mike.

"Exactly what I'm thinking," said Jake, turning off his phone and picking up the coded one they had been given.

"I'm glad our friend, Tomas, swept this room for bugs, too."

"Amen to that," said Jake, as he placed a call to Jason Bates. "Sorry to wake you, Jason, and sorry to disappoint you, but we won't be coming home . . . and I don't think the President will be unhappy with our new plans."

"I got it. I got it," said Bates. "Your gut was right again. Just give me the details so I can brief the President. It's 2:00 A.M. I don't need speeches!"

CHAPTER 33

Tomas had taken them to the airport and they said their goodbyes.

"Thank you for everything, Tomas," said Jake, extending his hand.

"We appreciate all you've done," said Mike, "and we are truly sorry about Diego."

Tomas shook their hands. "Mr. Sullivan . . . Mr. Lang . . . do me a favor. Find whoever did this . . . all of them . . . and end it. This evil has gone on for decades, and it grew in part in the land that I hold dear. If I can be of any help, let me know."

"You've got it, Tomas," said Mike. "You watch your back."

"Always," said Tomas, as he turned and headed for the exit.

Jake and Mike went through security, showing their passports, boarding passes, and diplomatic papers, and waited for the flight to Buenos Aires, where they would connect to a flight to Tampico, Mexico.

Once at the gate area for their flight, Jake said, "I've been thinking about something, Mike. What would make Gunselman move so quickly in 1954? He would have had to shut down his whole operation. He could only have done that with the approval of Group 45. We're assuming now he went to Mexico. Maybe he started over again."

"You think someone was closing in?"

"I do . . . and I think I know who it was . . . and I think we need to make another phone call . . . this time to an old friend of ours."

A woman carrying a baby and an old man with a tattered carry-all also waited at the gate, their eyes never leaving their prey.

CHAPTER 34

Like Jake and Mike at the airport, Lev Har-Even (alias Daniel Kosior) was sitting in a small café in Tunisia when his coded phone rang. He took it out and looked at the number and smiled.

"Mike Lang! I am honored to receive a call from the world's foremost sidekick! Is Jake with you?"

"You know, some day you and I are going to have to have a long discussion about that topic."

"I'd welcome it, my friend! What can I do for you?"

"Jake is here. We don't have a lot of time, Lev. We need some answers. How close were you to catching him in 1954?"

"What him? What are you talking about?"

"Look, we know the Mossad has been briefed on Group 45 and everything that's going on. Hell, you probably know where we are right now."

"Close." Lev Har-Even was making a decision as he sat in the café in Tunisia, and finally, he spoke. "Very . . . we missed him by only a couple of days."

"Gunselman?"

"Yes."

"Any idea where they went?"

"None. Vanished . . . into thin air."

"Any verification to a connection to Group 45?"

"One. In 1956 . . . when the Suez Crisis was ongoing . . . the British boarded a freighter off the coast of Egypt and found three dozen cases of illegal arms. They thought it was part of a plot to overthrow the Egyptian government."

"And?"

"And the boxes were all stamped 'Gunselman Gallery – San Carlos de Bariloche, Argentina'. I know you two well enough," he continued, "you've found something, haven't you? You're on the trail?"

"Maybe. So far it's a lot of maybe," said Mike, "but we'll see what we can do."

"Good hunting, my friends. Be careful."

"Always," said Mike, and he hung up. "We're definitely on the right track."

"Appears that way," said Jake, just as an older man approached them, holding his hat in front of him, both hands fingering the brim as he turned it round and round. "Can we help you, sir?" asked Jake.

He took out a handkerchief and wiped off his face as he sat his considerable girth in a chair across from them.

"Excuse me, Mr. Sullivan . . . Mr. Lang. Excuse my lack of manners. My name is Albrect Mercht. I missed an opportunity to speak with you before you left our beautiful city."

"Speak about what, Herr Mercht?"

"I assure you, it is more about what I can do for you."

CHAPTER 35

"And just what might that be?" asked Mike.

"I'm an old man, Mr. Lang, and have seen many things. I have been involved in the German community in Bariloche for many years. I am a chronicler."

"You don't say?" added Jake.

"I have something in my archives that might interest you."

"Go on."

"May I?" he said, reaching inside his coat.

"Carefully," said Mike.

He nodded and pulled out an envelope. Just then, a waitress came up and asked if she could get them anything. Jake and Mike both passed. Herr Mercht did not.

"A coffee, my dear. Plenty of cream and sugar," and he settled back in his seat.

After his coffee arrived, he began.

"Have you ever heard of Die Spinne?"

"It means 'the spider'," Mike said. "It was a Nazi organization used to bring your compatriots here to Argentina, like Odessa."

The old man sat bolt upright and slammed his fist on the table, the contents of his coffee splashing over the side, forming a pool in the saucer beneath it.

"They are *not* my compatriots! I am a German! I was never a Nazi! And you are wrong, Mr. Lang. Die Spinne was and is not just any organization. It was a commando unit created by one Otto Skorzey, and became a ruthless arm of Odessa, a killing arm. Odessa was the planning operation. It set up all the networks, the Ratline, the travel and business arrangements. Skorzey ran the assassination teams, smugglers, and mercenaries. Do you know how he made his way to Argentina, gentlemen? He was waiting in a cell . . . waiting to testify at Nuremberg . . . but on July 27, 1948, he escaped from his cell with the help of former SS officers. SS officers dressed as United States military police. Oh, yes, he often bragged how the United States authorities, one in particular, had aided his escape and supplied the uniform and planned the whole thing."

Jake and Mike looked at each other.

"But I digress from my purpose. I merely came to give you a photo, taken at a hacienda on the outskirts of Bariloche in 1951. Once it was discovered that the photo was taken, the cameraman was escorted out and never seen again. They destroyed the camera and threw the film out into the snow."

"But you were there, weren't you?" asked Jake. "And you retrieved the film, didn't you?"

Mercht smiled and nodded.

"And I developed it myself . . . so as far as the world has been concerned all these years, that film disappeared from the face of the earth. So, here, gentlemen, is a gift from a proud German and a hater of the Nazi cult and all it stands for," and he handed over the photo.

Jake and Mike took it and bent low to guard against the reflection from the overhead lights. The picture was faded over time, but it was clear enough, and it told a story.

Mercht spoke up.

"I thought you might recognize some people. The man and woman to the left, you might recognize as Juan and Eva Perón. Next to Mrs. Perón is her bodyguard, one Otto Skorzey, and next to him, Mr. Stephan Gunselman and his wife, Gretta. And the last gentleman, I believe you know."

Indeed, they did. The last gentleman was Judge Edmund C. Branson.

CHAPTER 36

"I find it strange, and you gentlemen might, also," said Mercht, "that even though Skorzey was Mrs. Perón's bodyguard . . . whom does he seem to be protecting? Look at his relationship to the parties. He seems to be much more concerned about Herr Gunselman, does he not?"

With difficulty, Herr Mercht raised his great heft from the seat and stood erect, took the hat he had been holding and put it on his head at a cocky angle, and smiled.

"Thank you for the coffee and the time, my friends. I hear facial recognition software can do wonders these days. I wish you well."

And with that, Herr Mercht made his way into the crowd.

CHAPTER 37

The next call didn't come until they were in the airport at Buenos Aires, waiting for their flight to Tampico, Mexico.

"Sam must have made another discovery," said Jake.

"Mr. Sullivan, I think I've found it. In late 1954, a new gallery and import and export center in fine arts opened in Tampico, Mexico, owned by one Hans Strausser, who died in 1976 at the age of 87. The business then passed to his son, Alios Strausser, who still runs it."

Jake looked at Mike.

"Alios . . . it can't be another."

"The Straussers appear to have been big in the Tampico social scene, but I found no photos on record yet."

"I have something for you, too, Sam," said Jake. "I'm going to email you a photo. After you look at it and do your magic, you'll recognize everyone there, except one person. That person is Stephan Gunselman, the owner of the Gunselman Gallery that closed in Bariloche in 1954. When you get it, run it all, and see what you come up with."

"Will do, Mr. Sullivan. Oh, and one other thing, the son's name, 'Alios' . . . that was the first name of Adolf Hitler's father."

CHAPTER 38

"We've found him, Mike. No doubt in my mind."

"But we haven't found the key yet."

"It's there. I know it's there. We're getting close."

Just then, the call came over the speakers for their 5:45 P.M. flight. It was going to take them approximately 22½ hours, including the two stopovers, and would get them to Tampico at 1:20 P.M. the following day.

"Here we go," said Mike, "another long flight."

Jake laughed.

"C'mon, Mike. All that means for you is another long sleep."

"That's why I have you, Jake," said Mike, walking away. "You stay up and do all that thinking, and I'll make sure I'm rested so that I can execute your plan."

As they headed for their plane, they were unaware that they were under the intense scrutiny of two of their fellow passengers, once again.

TAMPICO, MEXICO

CHAPTER 39

The long flight to Tampico was uneventful, and they landed on time and collected their baggage and made their way to 'Transportation'. There were two or three cabs available, and Mike nudged Jake and headed for one when a small, wiry Mexican with a bushy mustache, shaggy hair, and a faded LA Dodgers baseball cap stepped in front of them.

"Buenos dias, señors. My name is Jorge, and I can provide you the best rate for all your travel needs in Tampico and the rest of our beautiful country. Vacation, business, or pleasure . . . whatever it is you need, I will provide. Always prompt and at your beck and call . . . for the most reasonable price in the city."

Mike looked at Jake.

"I think we're okay," and he headed toward the cab he had noticed before.

Jorge moved closer to Jake.

"Please, señor. As you can see," looking around the transportation area, "business is slow. How long are you here for?"

"We really don't know," said Jake, starting to move away.

"I'll tell you what," said Jorge, "for thirty dollars American a day, I will provide you exclusive service . . . take you wherever you need to go . . . wait for you . . . pick you up whenever you want . . .

drop you off whenever you want . . . and be available just for you the whole time you're here."

Mike stepped forward after looking at Jake and seeing him smile.

"I tell you what, pal . . . twenty dollars a day and you've got a deal."

"Twenty-five and I'm yours," said Jorge.

"Done," said Mike.

"Please, my cab is over here. Where can I take you gentlemen?" said Jorge, moving quickly to one of the cabs in the row.

"The Holiday Inn," said Jake. "You know where it is?"

"Of course, of course," said Jorge. "It is on Calle Cristóbal Colón Zona Centro. A good choice, gentlemen . . . a good choice. In the heart of the city."

Jorge opened the doors for them, stashed their bags in the trunk, and got in and pulled away.

"You see, gentlemen, air conditioned. All the comforts. I will be the vehicle for you to enjoy your trip here in this beautiful city."

The truth be told, Jorge wasn't a bad tour guide. He explained how the town on the Panuco River became the chief oil export-ing port of the Americas in the early Twentieth Century and the second busiest port in the world.

"As you can see, gentlemen," he said, driving through the central Plaza de Armas, the beautiful architecture here came as the city grew under the rule of President Diaz. Our beautiful city has been compared to Venice, Italy, and New Orleans in your United States. Notice the wrought iron balconies on all the buildings," he said as they passed through the Plaza de la Libertad. He gradually arrived on the Calle Cristóbal Colón in Central City and pulled the cab to the curb. "Here you are, gentlemen . . . your destination." He opened the doors for them to get out and gave their bags to a bell-man. "Now, gentlemen, what else can I do for you today?"

"I think we're done for tonight, Jorge," said Jake. "We could both use a good shower, good meal, and then a good night's rest."

"I presume your travels were long, señor. From where did you come?"

"Buenos Aires," said Jake.

"Ahh, a long trip, indeed," said Jorge. He looked like he was thinking about something. "Gentlemen, it would be my honor, if you would allow me, to take you to dinner this evening. I know a very good restaurant near here . . . the La Pequena Nueva Orleans. Very good food . . . very good. Please, allow me."

Jake looked at Mike, who shrugged his shoulders.

"All right. Thank you, Jorge. We appreciate it. We'll be ready in an hour. How will that be?"

"I will wait. No problem. And then we will go."

CHAPTER 40

The hot showers did wonders for both Jake and Mike, and they realized they were both famished and went downstairs to find Jorge sitting in the lobby, hat in hand.

"You feel better, señors?"

"Much," said Jake.

"Let us go, let us go. Now you need that good meal you spoke of."

Once again, Jorge held the doors open and they entered the cab, even though they could have walked – the restaurant was only three-tenths of a mile from the hotel.

Although the food at the "Little New Orleans" was average at best, neither Jake nor Mike wanted to insult their host and made up for the quality of the meal by enjoying its quantity, which was reasonable by any standard. To be safe, they had opted for milkshakes, which came watered down, and burgers and fries, which were large and filling, if nothing else.

During dinner, Jorge had explained how he had been born on the outskirts of the city, had not had much schooling, and had taken over cab-driving duties from his late uncle, who had raised him, along with his wife. Jorge was gregarious and often funny, and all in all, it was a good evening and both Jake and Mike were glad that they had made their arrangements with the "vehicle" for their travels in the city.

Upon arriving back at the hotel, they made arrangements with Jorge for the following day.

"We need to get to the Strausser Art Gallery near the docks."

Jorge sat, rubbed his chin, and shook his head affirmatively.

"Yes, yes, I believe I know where it is. I will double check and make sure I have the proper directions. What time do you wish to leave?"

Jake looked at Mike and asked, "Ten o'clock all right?"

"The sooner the better," said Mike.

"Ten it is," said Jake.

"Agreed," said Jorge. "I will be here promptly to pick you up, gentlemen. Get a good night's rest."

"Thank you," said Jake. "And Jorge, thank you for dinner. It was very enjoyable," and he handed Jorge a twenty and a ten.

"But, señor . . ." started Jorge.

"We're good. See you in the morning."

"I told you Jorge would take care of you, didn't I?" said the cab driver. "I bid you goodnight, gentlemen. I will see you in the morning."

"Goodnight, Jorge," they said, waving, as they entered the hotel.

CHAPTER 41

Jake and Mike walked past the front desk and said goodnight to the young girl whose nametag said she was "Lucia", who had originally checked them in, and took the elevator to their floor. Had they stopped at the front desk and turned and looked out the entrance-way, they would have seen directly across the street a man who had been sitting at the bar in "Little New Orleans" during their dinner, and who was now watching the Holiday Inn and would do so from various positions throughout the night.

"Nice little guy, isn't he?" said Jake.

"I've got to admit, I was a little leery of the come-on," said Mike, "but I guess he's just trying to make a buck like everybody else. He sure as hell didn't have to buy us dinner, especially with what the cost probably means to him. I think when all is said and done we should probably go back to the original deal he wanted and give him his thirty bucks a day."

"Your soft spot is showing through, Mike."

"Hey, fair is fair. Sentiment has got nothing to do with it."

"Of course not," said Jake. "And I already did go back to the original deal."

Their rooms were on the same floor, and as Jake stopped at his door, he looked at Mike.

"You ready for tomorrow?"

"You really think we're going to find it, don't you?"

"I do," said Jake, "but I've no idea what we're going to encounter to get there."

"Don't worry, we're always ready for anything, right?"

"We have been so far."

"You worry too much, Jake. All will be well. Now get a good night's sleep."

"I'd tell you the same, but I know you will. That's a given."

"Some of us are just lucky," said Mike as he headed down the hall. "Goodnight."

Jake laughed to himself as he entered his room, hoping that he would get a night's rest like he knew his partner would.

CHAPTER 42

Sleep had come to Jake easily, and he was up early, fully rested, showered, and shaved. He checked and rechecked his weapon and put it in the holster in the back of his belt and then clipped the encrypted phone on the belt, also.

Judging by the weather the previous day, he knew it was going to be hot and opted for a short-sleeved shirt he could wear outside and a pair of chinos. He headed down the hall to get Mike.

As usual, Mike had slept like a baby so there was no need to ask, and Jake knew he would be armed and ready.

The two friends made their way down to the lobby and went into the small café, where they had a quick continental breakfast and then went outside to wait for Jorge.

It was a morning of brilliant sunshine, with a gentle breeze moving the trees at their very tops.

Jorge arrived promptly at ten o'clock, and it was only a short drive to the Maritime Custom House, north of the Panuco River, where the major Puerto de Tampico stretched out before them, only ten miles from the river's opening on the Gulf, and the ship-yards, canneries, sawmills, clothing manufacturers, machine repair shops, and import/export companies were already abuzz with activity, dealing in sugar, cattle, copper, coffee, petroleum, agave, and hides with the rest of the world.

"It is just up here on the left," said Jorge, as they entered a side street off the main dock area. They arrived at their destination, a well-kept building with the same balcony style seen in downtown with wide-shuttered upper windows, wrought iron balconies, and with a broad double wooden door with a sign in brass alongside, announcing "Strausser Galleries – Fine Art – Importing and Exporting".

CHAPTER 43

Jake asked Jorge to wait for them as he and Mike went inside. There they found a slightly portly man with thinning hair and wire-rimmed glasses sitting on the edge of his nose, looking over what appeared to be bills of lading at a small desk set in the corner of a room that was otherwise occupied by easels with various works of art and unopened crates off to the side, waiting to be either opened or shipped. The man rose from the desk somewhat unsteadily and used a cane to haltingly make his way to where Jake and Mike were standing.

"Gentlemen," he said, extending his hand. "I am Alios Strausser, the proprietor of this establishment," lifting the cane and moving it around the expanse of the room. "How may I help you?"

"Pleased to meet you, Mr. Strausser. My name is Jake Sullivan. This is Mike Lang. We are here on behalf of the United States Treasury Department. We are investigating complaints of forged paintings of European masters making their way into Central America and Mexico and then being trafficked in the United States. We were informed that your importing and exporting company was one of the most active along the Mexican coast and we wanted to find out whether or not you have heard anything relative to such activities or any other information you might be able to give us for our investigation."

Strausser pointed with his cane to two chairs in front of his desk.

"Come, gentlemen, sit," he said, as he again clumsily made his way over and around the desk and plopped down heavily on his seat of worn-out leather. He struck a pensive pose, as if he was seriously deliberating and searching for information that he could not otherwise recall. "I don't believe I have heard anything about such a situation, gentlemen. I'm afraid I can't be of much help."

Mike took out a pad and began writing.

"How long have you been here, Mr. Strausser?"

"This business was originally started by my father in the early 1950's. After his death, the business became mine, so we've been in operation continuously since that time."

"I notice your name," said Jake. "You're obviously not Mexican."

"No, no, I am not," laughed Strausser. "Not even close. No, my father emigrated to Mexico from Europe during the last great war."

He again used his cane to point to a photo behind him.

"This is my father . . . the founder of this enterprise."

"What does your business consist of?" asked Mike.

"We do a great deal of importing and exporting. We have connections with galleries all over the world, and we buy and sell back and forth for clients here and abroad who are interested in acquiring paintings once they go on the market."

"Sounds interesting," said Jake.

Strausser again laughed.

"It used to be much more so. Unfortunately, the internet and computers have taken the romanticism out of this business, and artwork is now bought and sold like any other commodity."

Jake looked at Mike and stood and headed toward the section of the room where the crates were stored.

"Are all of these coming into Mexico, or are they leaving?"

"Both," said Strausser, again getting up with difficulty and following Jake to the area in question. As he did so, his back was to his desk, and Mike quickly took out his phone and snapped a picture of the photo of Strausser's father that hung on the wall.

"Well, from the size of your operation, Mr. Strausser, it appears that your business is as we heard it was."

"I'm afraid that a lot of that is simply competitors who are jealous of our success, but we do what we can. I've tried to honor my father and keep the business running as he would have want it run."

Mike had also gotten up and moved over to the area with the crates.

"Well, Mr. Strausser, if there's nothing further you can tell us, I think we're done."

"Yes," said Jake, holding out his hand, "we thank you for your time. If you do think of anything, we are staying at the Holiday Inn here in Tampico for a while and would ask that you contact us."

"Absolutely," said Strausser. "If I can do anything at all, I will certainly do so. Criminal activity in this profession should not be tolerated. We are dealing in things of beauty that better mankind, and there's certainly no place for criminal enterprise in the midst of that."

After their goodbyes, Jake and Mike exited the building and found Jorge waiting. Once they were in the cab, Jorge turned.

"Where to now, gentlemen?"

"Drive around the block, if you would," said Jake. "I want to see if there's an alley behind this building and get some idea of its size."

"On our way," said Jorge, as he pulled out, went one block, made a left, and then another left into an alley half-way down from the intersection.

"Look," said Jake to Mike, "the front of the shops all appear to be of different types, but this wall runs almost the whole length of the alley. It's a huge warehouse behind at least one of those fronts."

"Yeah, and I can only guess which one," said Mike. "I think you're right, Jake. I think Alios is our boy. Think we need to pay another visit?"

"Not yet," said Jake. "There's one other place I want to go. I have a hunch about that investment that the Branson Foundation made, and I want to check it out. Jorge, can you take us to a place called the Metro?"

"Certainly," said Jorge. "A beautiful place. A museum of art and culture giving a history of our area. A very good place to go, very good."

"Well, that's our next stop," said Jake, looking at Mike, "and, hopefully, our last one."

Back in the Strausser offices, Alios Strausser was in the midst of a phone call.

"They were here. I did as you told me yesterday. As I've told you several times, I don't have the information necessary to open it. That is something only Simon had. I told you, the last time he was here, he changed the locking mechanism. I was told that there were workmen that came in, specially sent from the United States, who seemed to be there to install some type of electrical system. I have tried. I have had no luck in tracking down who they were or where they came from. You know the time frame as well as I do. It was right after he fled the United States and before he got to Paris." He almost spat, "Why do you not let me take care of these two? Why do you think they can find a way? Do you think they have magical powers? More American hubris. Yes . . . yes . . . I know who's in charge . . . yes . . . I will try again. I will let you know if there is any further contact. Goodbye."

"*What have you left me with, father?*" he said to himself. "*What have you left me with?*"

CHAPTER 44

On their way to the Metro, Jake and Mike had asked Jorge to pull over near an outside stand where, as in the rest of the known world, a vendor was selling cold Coca-Cola. Jake quickly got out and bought three, one for each of them, while Mike went into a nearby café to use the facilities.

As Jake and Mike returned to the cab, they could see Jorge speaking in an animated fashion on the phone. As he saw them approach, Jorge hung up, obviously agitated, and opened the doors for them.

"Is there a problem, Jorge?" asked Jake.

"Just dispatchers that don't want to understand things that you tell them. I explained to them that I had my vehicle rented for the entire day, and he's wondering why I'm not checking in for additional fares. When we made our arrangement, I called the dispatcher on duty then and told them."

"Don't worry, Jorge," said Jake, "we're making it worth your while."

"I know, and I appreciate it, but would you mind telling my dispatcher that?"

"Not at all," said Jake, and Jorge punched in a number on his phone.

There was a gruff, "Who is this?"

"This is Jake Sullivan. I'm Jorge's . . ." and he looked at Jorge for a last name.

"They'll know who you mean," said Jorge.

". . . fare for the day. We need him to take us to various places today. Is that going to be a problem?"

"No, no . . . not at all," said the voice, thick with a Mexican accent. "There must have been some confusion."

"Well, as I understand it," said Jake, "the confusion was yours, and I hope my call eliminates it."

"Absolutely . . . absolutely, sir. Have a good day."

"Thank you," said Jake, and handed the phone back to Jorge. "I don't think you're going to have any more problems."

"Thank you, señor . . . thank you. I appreciate it very much. Still to the Metro?"

Jake looked at Mike and said, "Let's go back to the hotel first. We'll report to Bates and see what's going on."

"There's also something I need to send," said Mike, showing Jake his phone.

"Jorge . . . back to the hotel it is," and they retraced their path until they arrived at the Holiday Inn.

"Jorge," said Mike, handing him some money, "go and get yourself some lunch and then come back. By then we should be ready to head to the Metro."

"Thank you, señors. I am somewhat hungry! I will return shortly!"

"Thank you, Jorge," said Mike. "Take your time."

CHAPTER 45

They went into Mike's room and Mike sent the photo of Strausser's father to Sam Walsh.

Next, Jake was on the phone with Jason Bates.

"So, you're still just going with your gut, huh?" asked Bates.

"No real proof yet. Hopefully, the photo we sent to Sam Walsh will get us that proof. Sam told us it's going to take a couple of hours, so we're going to wait it out here at the hotel, and as soon as I know anything, I'll let you know."

"Am I missing something, Jake? Even if you are right, how does that get us any closer to the key?"

"Because, Jason, if I'm right, one of the most evil men in the history of the world used the façade of art and refinement to run the same organizations he did in Germany on behalf of Group 45 to send armaments and assassins throughout the world. If Strausser is Gunselman, and if Gunselman and Judge Branson were in the company of Perón in Argentina, it proves he was in the center of it all. And if he was in the center of it all and fled Argentina to here, the key is here. We're almost there, Jason . . . just a little more time . . . that's all we need."

There was a long sigh from the other end of the phone call.

"I hope to God you're right, Jake. Group 45 is on a rampage, and we need to stop it. The President is counting on you, and so am I."

"We won't let you down. I'll call back when I know more."

"Sounds like Jason still isn't convinced," said Mike.

"No, but I am. Jorge should be done with his lunch. I'm going down and tell him we'll give him a call when we need him . . . that we have to wait here a little while. Hopefully, Sam won't take too long."

Jorge was again sitting patiently in the lobby, hat in hand, and stood up as soon as he saw Jake approach.

"A little change in plans, Jorge. We have to take care of some business . . . probably won't be able to leave until later this afternoon. Can you give me a number where I can reach you, and I'll give you a call?"

"Certainly, señor . . . no problem," said Jorge, as he moved to the front desk to ask for a piece of paper and pen and wrote down his number. "Call whenever you are ready, and I will be here."

"Thank you, Jorge, I appreciate it . . . and I apologize for the change in plans."

"No problem, señor, no problem. Maybe I can hustle up some other business while I wait," said Jorge, with a smile.

"I'm sure you can," said Jake. "I'm sure you can."

And with that, Jorge was out the door, humming a tune, and heading for his cab.

CHAPTER 46

Sam Walsh was wrong. It had taken only an hour for him to get a hit from the facial recognition software he was using on the photographs he had been provided. He couldn't believe the answer it had given him, but he knew it was correct, and he knew he had to call Jake Sullivan.

"It didn't take as long this time, Mr. Sullivan. I used the facial recognition package on the photographs you had given me before and added the new one to it. You found him, sir. According to the recognition software, there's a ninety-five percent chance that Gunselman and Strausser were the same man, and that man was Adolph Hitler."

Jake nodded at Mike.

"So all the conspiracy theorists had it right?" said Jake.

"They had theories, sir. You have fact," said Walsh. "You've unraveled one of the greatest mysteries of the Twentieth Century. I think it's just amazing."

"Thanks, Sam. Thanks for all your help. We appreciate it."

"And being part of this," said Sam, "I've never had anything like this happen before in my life. Believe me, the thank yous are all mine."

"Well, thank you anyway," said Jake. "Now I have to call Bates."

"Understood. If you need anything else, let me know," said Sam, and with that, he was gone.

"Jason," said Jake, "you're on speaker. Mike's here with me."

"And?" came the reply, and Mike just shook his head, laughing.

"And," he said, "I don't want to hear you make any more comments about Jake Sullivan's gut."

There was silence.

"You're telling me it's him?"

"It was him," said Jake. "Ninety-five percent certainty on the facial recognition software. Strausser was Gunselman, and Gunselman was Hitler. Here in Tampico, it's the center of everything, Jason. We're on the right track."

"Congratulations! You know, I never really doubted you."

"Really?" asked Mike.

"Yes, Lang, really. What's the next move?"

"We're heading out to the Metro later today."

"The Metro?" asked Bates.

"Yeah," said Mike, "the art gallery where Simon Branson made a $250,000.00 donation, and we're thinking it was for something more than a couple oil paintings."

"Such as what?" asked Bates.

"I think Branson bought himself some space," said Jake. "I'm not sure how or why, but I think that space holds what we're looking for. We have to find it and get in it, and, hopefully, we'll find the key."

"Well, let's hope you're right, again. Keep me posted," and the line went dead.

"The man's bursting with confidence," said Mike.

"Don't worry," said Jake, "it's there, and we're going to find it."

CHAPTER 47

Later in the afternoon, Jake placed a call to Jorge to meet them outside the Holiday Inn at approximately 5:00 P.M. As usual, he was right on time, and they headed to the Metro.

As Jorge explained, the Metro was really an entire cultural area, primarily dedicated to the Huasteca culture.

Leaving the urban sprawl of Tampico, they entered a green space surrounding a lagoon, the Laguna del Carpintero, and parked in a parking area and took a footbridge across the lagoon to the Cultural/Convention Center that housed a small museum. The entire area was filled with vendors selling food and gifts as children laughed to see the crocodiles splashing in the lagoon. They asked Jorge to wait for them outside the Center while they went in and looked around.

"We should be back in an hour," said Jake. "Just stay in this general vicinity so we can find you when we need you."

"No problem, señor. I will be here," said Jorge. "I have no need of the vendors," he said, patting his stomach. "What you bought me was very filling. I thank you again."

"No problem," said Mike, as he walked past him. "We'll see you shortly." And he and Jake entered the Center.

Fortunately, they realized immediately that they were out of place, as a string quartet played in a corner of the main lobby and men and women in evening attire and fine jewelry mingled with their tuxedoed counterparts at what was obviously some type of event.

Jake and Mike skirted the gala and moved down a passageway, past several exhibits dedicated to Mexico's Indian culture, without finding anything unusual. They turned a corner and saw a door at the end of a hallway.

"If I'm right," said Jake, "this should be at one end of the building."

Making their way down the tiled floor as quietly as they could, they reached the end, where there was what appeared to be a steel reinforced door with a plaque to one side that said, "In Memory of Judge Edmund C. Branson". Beneath the plaque were a screen and pad that Mike examined.

"Sophisticated set up," he said. "Voice and fingerprint recognition."

Just then, the sound of footsteps and the tapping of a cane echoed behind them. Reaching behind their backs for their weapons, they turned to see Alios Strausser approaching them in a black Armani tuxedo of the latest cut.

"Gentlemen, he said, had I known you were interested in our artifacts, I would have invited you to the gala. Can I help you with something?"

"Do you work here, Mr. Strausser?" asked Mike.

Strausser laughed.

"Not quite, Mr. Lang. I am the curator here."

"Good," said Jake, "maybe you can help us out. A good friend of mine told me that while I was here in Tampico, I should come and find an exhibit he had dedicated to his father. And," he said, looking at the plaque, "we've found it . . . but I don't think we can get in."

Strausser looked at the plaque.

"You knew this Judge Branson?"

"Actually, I did. His son and I grew up together."

"Really?" said Strausser. "What an amazing coincidence."

"It would seem that way," said Jake. "As I said," pointing to the locking mechanism, "it doesn't appear we can get in. Is there any way you could help us?"

"I'm sorry. That door hasn't been opened for many months, and I'm afraid it won't be in the future."

"Why is that?" asked Mike.

"Only the benefactor, Judge Branson's son, Simon, as you know, can open that door. And as I'm sure you also know, Mr. Branson met an untimely death not long ago in Paris."

Strausser was staring at them, and it was clear he knew who they were and the truth of the situation, but Jake and Mike kept up the charade.

"Well, thank you for your time, Mr. Strausser. Hope we will meet again before we leave."

"I'm sure we will," said Strausser. "I'm sure we will," and he turned and exited.

"Well, if he's telling us the truth, now what do we do?"

"I have an idea," said Jake. "Let's get back to the hotel and make some plans."

"This place will be under guard from now on," said Mike.

"I don't think so. Strausser's an arrogant son-of-a-bitch. I don't think he likes being someone who has to take care of details. I think he's convinced that lock can keep out anybody."

"And you don't think so?"

"Like I said, Mike, I have an idea."

They exited the Metro and found Jorge dutifully waiting for them and had him drive them back to the Holiday Inn.

CHAPTER 48

Back at the hotel, Jake was on the phone with Bates, explaining what they had found, and when he told Bates what they needed, he quickly switched them to Stanley Cashman, the tech that had given them the equipment to infiltrate the computer, along with Jake's coded phone.

"All right, Stan, here's what we're facing. I no longer have any doubt that the key is here and it's inside that room, but we need to get in. From the best we can tell, it requires voice and fingerprint recognition."

"Let me see what I can do," said Cashman. "We have Branson's fingerprints on file here, and, I might add, only here. Any possible places for those fingerprints to be registered have been found and they have been destroyed, and every place where we knew he was has been thoroughly scrubbed."

"How did you know what we were going to find?"

"That type of entry system is pretty common today. We just weren't taking any chances."

"So, you've been working on the voice recognition, also?" asked Jake.

"Playing around a little. Let me see what I can come up with. I think we can help you out."

"That's what I was hoping you'd say," said Jake. "Let us know."

"As quickly as I can," said Cashman, and the line went dead.

CHAPTER 49

Night had fallen when the call came through. Jake put the call on speaker.

"I'm sending information to your phone. There are copies of all Branson's fingerprints and I also isolated him speaking his name. Hopefully, it will work. Make sure the prints are on the scanner and close enough for the system to hear the sound. I've tried to erase all extraneous sounds to leave only the voice pattern and, hopefully, I've succeeded. Start with the right thumb print."

"Nice work," said Mike.

"Indeed. Thanks Stan," said Jake. "If you don't hear back from us, we're in."

"I'm here, too," said Bates. "Good luck. Maybe your gut will pay off once again, Jake."

"Someday you're going to learn, Jason."

"It's not a done deal yet, Lang," and Jason hung up.

Mike shook his head and said, "Always, always pleasant."

"Come on. We've got work to do," said Jake, and they headed out the door.

After Cashman's call, they had phoned Jorge, who arrived fifteen minutes after they had entered the lobby.

Jorge had already told them the Metro closed at 9:00 P.M., and they wanted to arrive just before closing.

"Come, gentlemen, I know a good roadside stand where you can get something in your bellies, and then I will take you to the Metro at the perfect time."

CHAPTER 50

The tacos had been amazingly good. They entered the Metro and quickly made their way down the hallway to a supply closet they had seen before. Mike was able to open it without much difficulty, even though it was locked, and they slipped inside.

The arrangement they had made with Jorge was to wait for two hours, and if they didn't appear, to call the Federales to come in after them.

Unknown to them, the man dressed all in black, perched in a tree across the lagoon with night-vision goggles, had watched the whole thing and made a call on his own coded phone. That call had caused the exchange of others, that ended with orders being given and action being taken.

Mike and Jake stayed in the storage closet for approximately forty-five minutes, and when they emerged, everything was dark in the hallway outside. They could see some lights coming from the lobby area where the main floor-to-ceiling windows were located, and which were obviously kept on into the night.

They used the penlights they had brought with them and moved down the hallway outside the storage closet and made two rights and found themselves in the hallway with the locked door at the end. There were no signs of anyone as they moved toward the door. When they arrived in front of it, Mike shined both penlights on the locking mechanism and Jake went to work. He looked at Mike.

"Keep your fingers crossed. Here goes nothing."

"My fingers are a little busy right now," said Mike. "Don't worry. We'll be all right."

Jake did as Cashman had directed and put the print of the right thumb on the sensor, at the same time pressing a button on his phone, which was held right next to the speaker, and the words came out: "Simon Branson". There was a click, and the lock opened.

CHAPTER 51

As they entered the room, Mike propped the door open with his penlight, unsure how the locking mechanism would work from the inside. Using the sliver of light from the hallway, Jake felt along the wall for a light switch, found it, and pressed it in. Dim ceiling lights came on in a semi-circle around the room. There was one bench in front of the far wall, and a spotlight was shining on a painting on that wall.

"What the hell is this?" said Mike.

They moved toward the painting and looked at it. A plaque on the picture frame had etched on it 'The Old Building In Stand Of Trees'.

"What's this about?" asked Mike.

"It's a painting . . . by Adolf Hitler. He painted it in 1909." said Jake, as he moved toward it. It was hung in a large gilded frame, and beneath it sat an ornate carved table on which was a beautiful bronze urn.

Mike walked along the semi-circle that formed the walls.

"Jake, there's nothing else here. What kind of gallery is this?"

"It's not a gallery," said Jake. "It's a crypt. It's a memorial. Simon did this for Hitler's son. This is his father's final resting place . . . right underneath his favorite work of art."

Mike walked over and said, "Are you saying . . . in there . . .?" and Jake shook his head.

"Hitler's ashes."

"So this has nothing to do with computers or the key or anything else? This was just a gift for all the evil Hitler had perpetrated in the name of Group 45 for Simon to get the son's loyalty?"

Jake didn't respond. He just kept staring at the painting, particularly at the frame. It stood out and protruded from the wall a much greater distance than was necessary for an average frame, and Jake began to feel the sides.

"Wait a minute . . . there's mesh up here . . . and a small screen below it. I think it's the same setup as the outside lock," and Jake repeated the steps with his phone, putting Branson's thumbprint on the scanner and having his name spoken into the mesh. Once again they heard a click, and the frame began to swing open, revealing an elaborate computer system built into the wall.

Jake immediately hit the preset button on his phone and was connected to Stanley Cashman and told him what they had done and what they had found.

"Describe it to me as best you can," said Cashman, and Jake did. "Look on the right-hand side, about three inches below the monitor. There should be a covered USB port there."

"I see it," said Mike, and took the cover off, Stan hearing what was going on by speaker.

"All right, insert the flash drive I gave you, and I'll tell you if we get a connection," and Mike did so.

"Yes!" came the voice from the other side. "We're in!"

"How long is this going to take?" asked Mike, looking back at the door, which they had propped open with Mike's penlight, not sure exactly how the mechanism would work to exit the premises.

"Don't worry, Mike," said Cashman, "we'll be in and out before you know it. Wow, there's a lot of data here. I should still be in and out in less than five minutes. Let me get started."

Mike went to guard the door while Jake sat on the bench staring at the computer. It actually took only four minutes before Cashman's voice came back on.

"Done. We've got it all, gentlemen. Great work."

"Did you take care of the erase?" asked Mike.

"Absolutely," said Cashman. "All the data is erased and the hard drive is fried. If this was the only system they had, they don't have any information anymore . . . only we do."

"Good work, gentlemen," came the voice of Jason Bates. "I've got to hand it to you . . . you did it again."

"Holy hell! Is that a compliment, Jason?" asked Mike, as he made his way to where Jake was standing.

"Don't let it go to your head," came the reply. "Now get out of there and get back home before something happens."

CHAPTER 52

Unfortunately, Bates's words came too late. Just then the door was pushed open and Alios Strausser hobbled into the room on his cane, a Beretta in his hand, held at waist level, pointed in the direction of Jake and Mike. He was accompanied by four men in paramilitary gear holding automatic weapons, with someone between them, and when the light finally showed who that someone was, Jake's legs almost buckled.

"Jake, what's wrong?" asked Mike.

"You . . . you're the leader of Group 45. I should have known," and he thought back to what Simon had said: 'She walks in beauty,' and Jake's mind drifted back to an old high school yearbook, where a picture of a beautiful girl had those words inscribed below it. Simon hadn't told him, "This killed me", he had said, "Sis killed me."

"Jake?" asked Mike, and Jake snapped out of his thoughts and looked at Mike.

"Mike Lang . . . meet the leader of Group 45 . . . Simon Branson's sister, Patty."

CHAPTER 53

"Jake, what the hell are you talking about? What's Group 45? These men have kidnapped me and brought me here!"

"Save it, Patty! And to think I trusted you. The whole time, when you called, wanting information . . . I should have seen it then. What's wrong with your family? This thirst for power . . . you killed your only brother and his wife!"

"Jake, I don't know what you're talking about! I didn't kill anyone! Simon and I have been estranged and haven't spoken to each other, but I loved him. I loved Susan."

"And to think that growing up, I looked up to your family . . . all of you . . . you're pure evil!"

"Jake, please!" said Patty, now crying. "I don't know what you're talking about! I . . ."

And she was cut off, as another four men entered the room and a voice shouted, "Enough! Enough of the drama!"

CHAPTER 54

Jorge strolled into the gallery, also holding a weapon, his a Glock 17.

"Will you two please stop! I can't take it anymore!"

"Jorge?" asked Mike, quizzically.

"Not exactly, Mr. Lang," said Jorge, only this time, the voice changed. He motioned to one of the men and said, "Search them for weapons," and Jake and Mike were relieved of their Glocks.

"Would someone please tell me what's going on?!" screamed Patty.

"Oh, shut up, Patty!" said Jorge, the voice changing even more, becoming almost feminine. "Blah, blah, blah . . . yes, you're not guilty . . . it wasn't you . . . you didn't know anything about this . . . we know, we know . . . and quite frankly, I don't need you anymore," and Jorge raised his weapon and put a bullet between Patty Branson's eyes.

"Patty!" screamed Jake, as she fell to the floor, blood seeping from the hole, and he headed toward Jorge but was blocked by the armed guards who roughly pushed him back. He just stood, looking in amazement.

As Patty lay there, Alios Strausser began to laugh. He looked at Jorge and said, "You see, Americans can die very easily."

Mike replied, "So can Germans, asshole! Just remember that little thing called World War II . . . when America destroyed all of the plans of the biggest piece of shit the world has ever known!"

"Silence!" yelled Strausser, now in a rage as he pointed his Beretta at Mike. "How dare you! This place is holy. Here rests the ashes of my father, the greatest man the world has ever known! Betrayed by others!" He sneered at Jake. "I would kill you, but I will not defile this place with more American blood!"

"Enough!" said Jorge. "Enough!" And he spoke to one of the men. "Go check it."

The man inserted a flash drive into the computer, just as Jake and Mike had done . . . the flash drive being connected to a small-screened device he stared at. He turned back to Jorge and shook his head. Jorge sighed, looked away, and shook his head, and turned back to Strausser, extending the Glock and aiming it straight at him.

"What are you doing?" said Strausser.

"You disobeyed my orders, Alios. You were supposed to put guards in place so that as soon as they opened the door, which I knew they would, they could stop them from getting to the computer . . . but you didn't . . . and now they've destroyed the most valuable information we had and have the ability to disrupt our entire organization . . . all because of you!"

"I didn't think these foolish Americans had the capability to open the door."

"Obviously, you were wrong."

Alios puffed out his chest.

"You won't shoot me. My father was Adolf Hitler! He performed great service to Group 45! He was a hero and a legend, and I am his son."

"Yes, you are," said Jorge, shaking his head, "but that's all ancient history, Alios. Group 45 has new boys running the show, and they all report to me, so it doesn't really matter who your father was, does it?" and he fired directly at the puffed out chest, knocking Strausser backwards until he collapsed at the base of the wall. "Goddamn pompous Germans," muttered Jorge under his breath.

"Who the hell are you?" said Jake, staring at Jorge.

"Oh, I'm sorry. Here, let me explain," and Jorge began to take off a wig, remove the fake mustache that had sat above his lips, took padding out of the cheek pouches, removed the bushy eyebrows, wiping makeup off his face.

Jake suddenly lurched to the bench. The guards moved to stop him, but Jorge waved them off.

"It's all right. Let him sit down. I believe our friend Jake has put it all together . . . haven't you, Jake?"

Jake sat down on the bench, and like Adolf Hitler had in his dying years, stared at a portrait he had painted. He wondered whether or not Hitler had wished that his life had taken a different turn and he had become the artist he wanted to be, rather than what he ultimately was.

It had all come together so quickly, like it always did . . . that crystal clear recognition of one thing that leads to the unraveling of the entire mystery. Jake wondered how he could have missed so much, and then he remembered Simon telling him, "*You have done more for my family than you'll ever know*," and he watched the transformation complete itself and the voice changed, and finally, before him, instead of Jorge, stood Joan Phoebe Taylor, daughter of Benjamin Matthews.

"Son-of-a-bitch!" said Mike. "It can't be!"

"Just bitch, if you please, Mr. Lang," said Taylor. "Oh, yes, it's me . . . in the flesh."

"But you're in prison."

"Obviously I'm not, Mr. Lang. You would be amazed how many people you can find who are willing to take your place, even in a prison cell, for guaranteed protection of their loved ones . . .

and a sufficient sum of money. And that young lady, who is allegedly me, would never give me up because of it . . . and no one else knows, except you. And, gentlemen, as much as I've enjoyed our sparring back and forth, this is the end. It's time for you both to go."

"But how the hell . . ." asked Mike, trailing off, looking at Jake.

"It's my fault, Mike. I missed it. I missed it all. It was so simple . . . so easy to figure out. It answers so many questions."

"She's the leader of Group 45?"

"Now she is. She won the battle with Simon."

"But I thought Simon told us he didn't want any part of it."

"He didn't," said Jake, "but he came to believe that he had to. Group 45 was going in a whole new direction. He might not have agreed with Judge Branson and what he did, but in his mind, he was doing the best thing for the country, at least in the beginning. But what Group 45 became under new leadership when Judge Branson died was nothing like the Judge's vision."

"But wait, when the Judge died . . . she's too young."

"That's the part I missed. When Simon called me in Florida after we discovered the documents at the mansion, remember what he told me?"

"Not really."

"He told me I had done more for his family than I could imagine."

"And?" said Mike.

"What I had done was take out the leader of Group 45 . . . the leader that Simon despised . . . the leader that Simon felt was destroying the vision of the Group that his father had." He looked over at Taylor. "Why Patty?"

"I needed the same things you did. I was trying to get close to Simon. At first I wanted to see if I could somehow bring him over to my side. When I found out that was an impossibility, I arrived at similar conclusions to yours concerning this room and what was in it. Simon had been smart. He changed the entry mechanism to both the door and the computer so that only he could get to it."

"Why didn't you take him alive, then?" asked Mike.

"That was the original plan. There was a war going on internally in Group 45. Lack of leadership will do that. A kill squad was sent out without my authority. You know the rest. Before, I had made calls to Simon. He thought it was Patty . . . and I was trying to bring brother and sister closer together. After all, you have to admit, you've seen my role as Jorge . . . I am a great actress. When I found out it wasn't working, I drove the wedge farther between them. He didn't know I existed. He wasn't looking for me. He thought he was dealing with his sister, who had turned on him, but he couldn't bring himself to do harm to her . . . not his own sister . . . so he had to act in other ways."

"And why all this?" asked Jake, motioning with his arms around him.

"Jake, don't underestimate yourself. I could never get that idiot to say the words 'Simon Branson' as hard as I tried. But I knew you would do it. You'd find the key for us . . . and you did. And if that asshole," pointing to Alios, slumped on the floor, "had done what he was told, it would now be ours. But, c'est la vie."

"Why you? Why the disguise?" asked Mike.

"Oh, I've had men tracking you . . . in your home town, Paris, Bavaria, everywhere. I couldn't take a chance. Like I've told you, there were some people who just wanted you dead, but I knew you couldn't let it go. I knew you'd figure it out, and I knew you'd start to hunt for the key. As we got down to the end of the adventure, I wanted to take care of you myself to make sure nothing happened to you . . . and also to be there for the crowning moment. But . . . you can't depend on people these days, Jake, so now we have to part and go our merry ways. I have new worlds to conquer, and, I'm afraid, that your world and that of Mr. Lang is at an end."

"At least I got rid of your father," said Jake.

Joan Taylor, who had been moving toward the exit, walked up to where Jake was sitting and put her face inches from his. He could see the hatred and rage in her eyes.

"And I vowed I would avenge him . . . an eye for an eye and all those other Biblical goodies. Truth be told, Jake, you two . . . I'm just tired of you," and she turned to walk out the door.

Mike said, "I still don't get it. Between the old man's death and this nut job, who ran this thing?"

Taylor turned around and smiled at Jake.

"Go ahead, Jake, tell him."

Jake's face never left Taylor's as he began to speak.

"A young protégé that the Judge probably met at some alumni meeting at Yale. A member of Skull and Bones, just like he was. Someone he took under his wing. Someone he saw promise in. And someone he never understood . . . didn't have an ounce of his courage, humanity, or his principles . . . as warped as they might be. Your father, Joan . . . Benjamin Matthews . . . the former leader of Group 45."

CHAPTER 55

"You've got to be kidding me," said Mike.

"Think about it," said Jake, "we always wondered how he had so much information . . . so much power . . . why he was able to do the things he did . . . escape from prison. He wasn't operating alone. He had this whole network behind him, and that's why Simon thanked me for putting him down."

Taylor looked at Mike and shook her head.

"You've got to admit, Mr. Lang, he's pretty good. All right, got to go, boys." She looked at the men lining the room. "When I'm gone, kill them, and seal the room," and she headed for the exit.

CHAPTER 56

Just after she departed, flash grenades were thrown into the room and exploded. Jake was knocked off the bench and he and Mike were thrown to the floor against the wall that contained the computer system. They barely heard silenced shots of various weapons going off, but smoke and cordite filled the room, and then there was silence. A man in full military gear came up to them and raised his goggles.

"You boys all right?" he asked, smiling.

"Nice to see you, Commander Donahower," said Jake.

"Yeah, nice timing, as usual," said Mike.

"Now," said Jake, "please explain to me how the hell you're here."

CHAPTER 57

"It was your buddy, Bates, and the President. He gave me a special assignment of watching over you two, and my men have been following you on this little adventure of yours. You were also being tailed by the bad guys. Our job was to protect you and make sure you stayed alive so you could get the information you were looking for."

"It was you who took out those two at the glacier," said Mike.

"One of my men was only too glad to help," said Donahower.

"I knew we didn't hit those guys," Jake said to Mike.

"Cut things a little close here, didn't you?" he then asked Donahower.

"Sorry about that, Mr. Sullivan. Group 45 is a tough outfit. They had a hell of a perimeter set up outside. We had to take them out, quietly, one by one, so we didn't alert the crew in here."

"But how did you know . . ." Jake began to ask.

"One of my men was outside and saw the troops arrive. He put in a call to me, I called Bates, and we got our orders. We were in an inflatable on the far side of the lagoon, and like I said, if not for the fight outside . . . My apologies for putting you so close to danger."

"Not necessary," said Jake. "We're still up and walking around . . . once again I might add."

"Yeah," said Mike, "apologies aren't necessary. It all worked out, and we ended up a lot better than they did," he said, pointing to the bodies lying around the room.

And then it hit Jake.

"Wait . . . Taylor . . . there was a girl here. She was dressed in men's clothes. She went outside just before you got here."

"Sorry, Mr. Sullivan. Never saw such a person."

"She must have gotten away just before you entered," said Jake, shaking his head.

"And so it continues," said Mike.

EPILOGUE

MIAMI, FLORIDA

CHAPTER 58

It was one year after the events in Tampico, Mexico, and Jake and Mike were back at their jobs in Miami.

If someone had been closely observing the news during that year, they would have noticed that mid and higher level officials in governments around the world were resigning or dying of natural causes or accidental deaths. Through a coordinated effort, most of the announcements were buried deep in the media flow where people didn't tend to go and the pattern was never recognized.

The key provided invaluable information and Group 45 was on the retreat, but the war wasn't over. Joan Taylor was still out there, still in control, and still with vast resources at her disposal.

Jake and Mike both knew they were in this for the long haul and the battle would go on.

CHAPTER 59

It was late in his office in Miami. Jake was just finishing up paper-work. They had cracked an arm shipments ring delivering supplies to the Middle East and it had reminded him of the crates Lev Har-Even had told them about early in the investigation. It was clearly the work of Group 45, and Jake had considered one more limb cut off the tree.

Mike walked in Jake's office.

"Still pushing papers, I see."

"Federal government, Mike. It lives on paperwork . . . you know that. But I'm almost done and getting ready to head out. How about you?"

"Yeah, I'm about done myself, but I had to show you something. I think we need to send this to Tomas. A buddy of mine at the FBI followed through on my old request. This was just declassified."

Jake took the paperwork and read it.

FEDERAL BUREAU OF INVESTIGATION

Form No. 1 THIS CASE ORIGINATED AT	LOS ANGELES			FILE NO. 105-410	
REPORT MADE AT LOS ANGELES	DATE WHEN MADE 9-21-45	PERIOD FOR WHICH MADE 8-5,7,10,11,14, 18,23,25,28,30; 9-1,5,15,18-45	REPORT MADE BY		
TITLE HITLER HIDEOUT	REPORT ON		CHARACTER OF CASE SECURITY MATTER - G		

SYNOPSIS OF FACTS: ▮▮▮▮▮▮ reports contact with ▮▮▮▮ (phonetic). Claims to have aided six top Argentine officials in hiding ADOLPH HITLER upon his landing by submarine in Argentina. HITLER reported to be hiding out in foothills of southern Andes. Information obtained by ▮▮ from ▮▮▮ unable to be verified because of disappearance. Attempts to locate ▮▮▮▮ negative. No record of him in police or INS files.

-C-

REFERENCE: Los Angeles letter to Bureau, 8-14-45

DETAILS:

▮▮▮▮▮▮▮▮▮▮ Hollywood, California, ▮▮ reported to a ▮▮▮▮ on the City Desk of the Los Angeles Examiner newspaper that upon his leaving the Melody Lane Restaurant at Hollywood and Vine on or about July 28, 1945, he met a friend of his who at the time was engaged in a conversation with an individual who later identified himself as ▮▮▮▮ (phonetic). ▮▮▮▮ friend whose identity he does not wish to disclose because of reasons that will later be explained, remarked to ▮▮ that he would like to have him meet ▮▮▮▮ as it was quite evident that ▮▮▮▮ had a problem on his mind. ▮▮▮ continued that after being introduced to ▮▮ his friend left and he spent several hours with ▮▮▮ and obtained the following information.

▮▮▮▮▮ disclosed to ▮▮▮ that he wished to find some high government official who would guarantee him immunity from being sent back to Argentina if he told him the following information. According to ▮▮▮ he

APPROVED AND FORWARDED:		SPECIAL AGENT IN CHARGE		DO NOT WRITE IN THESE SPACES	
COPIES OF THIS REPORT 5-Bureau 1-SID, Los Angeles 1-ZIO, Los Angeles 2-Los Angeles	COPIES DESTROYED R 207 NOV 1 1960				

105-410

was one of four men who met HITLER and his party when they landed from two
submarines in Argentina approximately two and one-half weeks after the fall
of Berlin. ████████continued that the first sub came close to shore about
11:00 p.m. after it had been signaled that it was safe to land and a doctor
and several men disembarked. Approximately two hours later the second sub
came ashore and HITLER, two women, another doctor, and several more men,
making the whole party arriving by submarines approximately 50, were aboard.
By pre-arranged plan with six top Argentine officials, pack horses were
waiting for the group and by daylight all supplies were loaded on the horses
and an all-day trip inland toward the foothills of the southern Andes was
started. At dusk the party arrived at the ranch where HITLER and his party,
according to ████████, are now in hiding. ████████ most specifically explained
that the subs landed along the tip of the Valdez Peninsula along the southern
tip of Argentina in the gulf of San Matias. ████████ told ████████ that there
are several tiny villages in this area where members of HITLER's party would
eventually stay with German families. He named the towns as San Antonio,
Videma, Neuquen, Muster, Carmena, and Rason.

████████maintains that he can name the six Argentine officials
and also the names of the three other men who helped HITLER inland to his
hiding place. ████████ explained that he was given $15,000 for helping in
the deal. ████████explained to ████████that he was hiding out in the United
States now so that he could later tell how he got out of Argentina. He stated
to ████████that he would tell his story to the United States officials after
HITLER's capture so that they might keep him from having to return to
Argentina. He further explained to ████████that the matter was weighing on his
mind and that he did not wish to be mixed up in the business any further.

According to ████████, HITLER is suffering from asthma and ulcers,
has shaved off his mustache and has a long "but" on his upper lip.

████████ gave the following directions to ████████ "If you will go
to a hotel in San Antonio, Argentina, I will arrange for a man to meet you
there and locate the ranch where HITLER is. It is heavily guarded, of course,
and you will be risking your life to go there. If you do go to Argentina,
place an ad in the Examiner stating, ████████ call Hempstead 8458,' and I
know that you are on the way to San Antonio."

The above information was given to ████████████████
████████, reporter on the Los Angeles Examiner on July 29, 1945.

The writer contacted ████████in an attempt to locate ████████n order
that he might be vigorously interviewed in detail concerning the above store.
████████reiterated the information set out above, adding that the friend to
whom ████████was talking in front of the Melody Lane Restaurant was a friend
of his by the name of "JACK," last name unknown, but that since the introduction
he has had further conversation with "JACK" and "JACK" advised him that while
he was eating his lunch at the Melody Lane Restaurant ████████sat at his table

-2-

3

LA 105-410

and after the meal followed him out where he engaged in a conversation in front of the restaurant. ██████ according to "JACK," had mentioned that he had important information to divulge and solicited his cooperation in locating the proper officials to whom to impart this information. "JACK" told ████ that it was at this time that ████ came along and he asked ████ to listen to his story inasmuch as he, "JACK," was in a hurry.

██████ added that he had spent several hours engaged in general conversation which he explained was a "feeler" on the part of ████ to determine if he, ████ was all right and could be relied upon. He then advanced the story which has been related above.

██████ advised that he told ████ he would try to help him, and for him to call back at the Hempstead number in a few days and he would have some information for him. ████ continued that he immediately contacted ████ at the Examiner and ████ tried to arrange a meeting with ████ and in the meantime inserted the story in the newspaper which, according to ████ evidently scared ████ stated that he was unable to throw any more light on the story inasmuch as all the information obtained from ████ is incorporated in the story. ████ according to ████, did not spell his name but simply introduced himself as ████ which is phonetic.

██████ was advised by the writer that if ████ telephoned him or if he was observed at any time to immediately engage him in conversation to explain that the proper authorities wished to discuss the matter further in detail with him personally. To date ████ has not contacted ████

██████ advised that he eats two meals daily at the Melody Lane Restaurant but he has not observed the subject since his first meeting. The writer has continually spot-checked the Melody Lane Restaurant at meal time in an effort to locate ████ with negative results.

The Hollywood and Los Angeles police records have been checked with negative results on the name ████ and other similar sounding names.

The records of Immigration and Naturalization Service were also checked with negative results under the name ████ and similar sounding names with negative results.

Because of the lack of sufficient information to support the story advanced by ████, it is believed impossible to continue efforts to locate HITLER with the sparse information obtained to date.

██████ tells an apparently reliable story but admits there is some doubt in his mind as to whether ████ is telling the truth.

A description of ████ obtained from ████ is as follows:

-3-

"Diego Cruz and his uncle were telling the truth . . . and Tomas needs to know just how much his friend helped us. Send it."

"Will do," said Mike. "Any plans for the weekend?"

"As a matter of fact, the girls are coming in."

"That's great!"

"Hey, why don't you come over on Sunday? We'll make some steaks, you can have a few beers . . . they'd love to see you."

"You're on."

"I'll call you later and let you know what time."

"Sounds good. Don't stay too late."

"Following you out the door," said Jake. And he did, and took the elevator down to the garage level. He got out and headed to his car.

He had just clicked the remote to unlock the vehicle when he felt the barrel of a gun at the back of his neck. The assailant was good . . . he hadn't heard a thing . . . hadn't seen a shadow . . . and assumed that Group 45 was there to finally finish the task.

"What are you waiting for?" said Jake.

"Mr. Sullivan, I'm going to lower this gun and you're going to turn around. I'm going to hand this weapon over to you."

"Not a very good plan for an assassination," said Jake.

"I don't mean you any harm," said the man. "I just want to talk to you. I tried to call you on numerous occasions, but I couldn't get through. What I have to tell you is important, and I just want you to listen . . . and I apologize for this, if I frightened you or upset you, but I need you to listen to me. Now, please turn around."

Jake did. He saw an older black gentlemen, medium height, casually dressed in jeans and a pullover, holding what appeared to be an old .38, which he now held out in the palm of his hand. Jake took it and checked it. It was empty.

"I have to tell you, Mr. . . . ."

"We'll get to that," said the unknown assailant.

"I don't like to be threatened."

"Again, Mr. Sullivan, I apologize. I gave you my reasons. Will you listen to me? Please?"

There was an earnestness in the man's voice, and Jake sighed and pressed the button to lock his car.

"Come on. We'll go up to my office. This better be good."

"Mr. Sullivan, are you aware of the name Meriwether Lewis?"

COMING FALL 2017

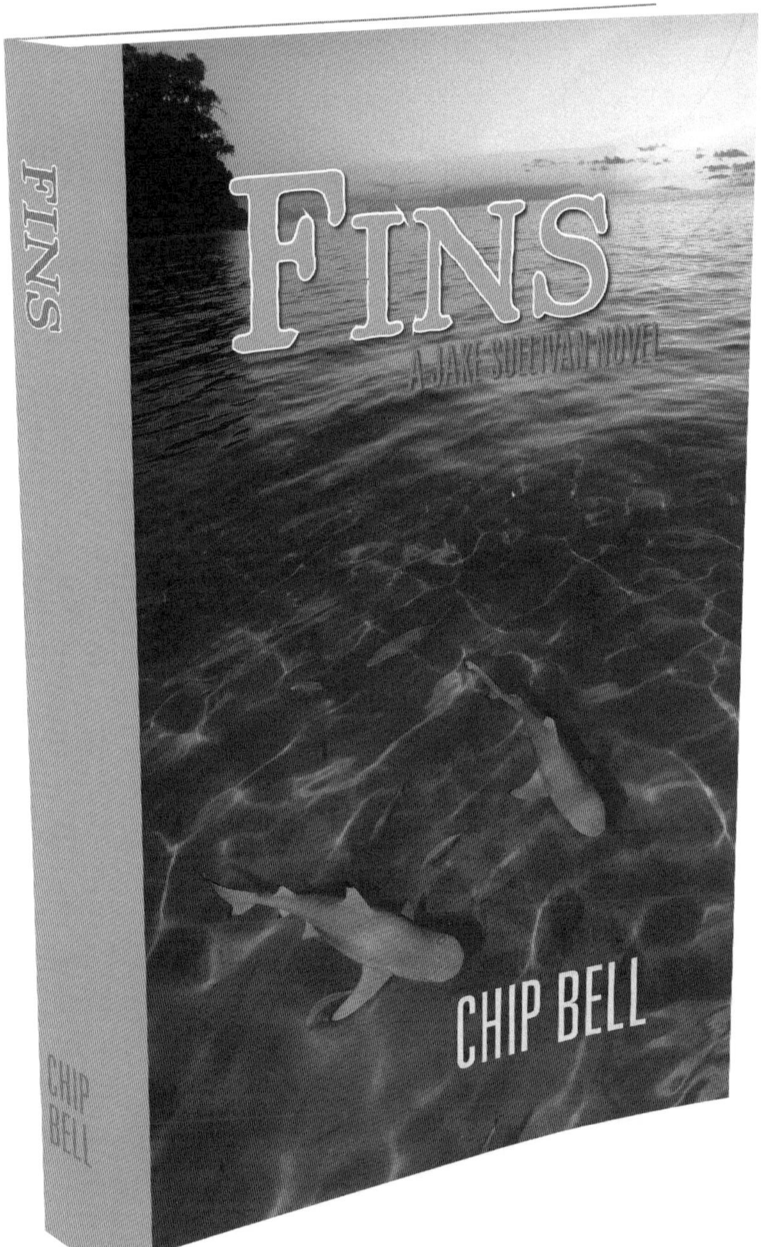
FINS
A JAKE SULLIVAN NOVEL
CHIP BELL
FINS
CHIP BELL

CHIP BELL

1725 FIFTH AVENUE
ARNOLD, PA 15068

724-339-2355

chip.bell.author@gmail.com
clb.bcymlaw@verizon.net
www.ChipBellAuthor.com

FOLLOW ME ON FACEBOOK
facebook.com/chipbellauthor

FOLLOW ME ON TWITTER
@ChipBellAuthor

FOLLOW ME ON PINTEREST
pinterest.com/chipbellauthor
/the-jake-sullivan-series

**TAKE THE TIME TO REVIEW
THIS BOOK ON AMAZON**
amazon.com/author
/chipbellauthor.com

WA